ONE HUNDRED HEARTBEATS

AN ASPEN COVE SMALL TOWN ROMANCE

KELLY COLLINS

BOOK NOOK PRESS

DEDICATION

To Jim, Nik, Alec, and Gabby. My heart beats for you.

CHAPTER ONE

There were three things Katie Middleton knew with absolute certainty:

Hope appeared in a pink envelope.

Prince charming rode a Harley.

Some secrets were better left unspoken.

Katie relaxed at her favorite table in the bakery—the one directly under the Wishing Wall—and checked items off her bucket list. It was unlike the list most people had with dreams like climbing Mount Kilimanjaro, running a marathon, or writing a book. Her list had the simple things she had never done, like flying a kite, rowing a boat, and baking a muffin.

Katie's life had been full of wishes for as long as she could remember, most of which had never materialized, so when she got a pink envelope with the deed to a bakery inside, she packed up her stuff and moved from Dallas, Texas, to Aspen Cove, Colorado.

It came as a shock to her family and friends when she disappeared without a word to a location she hadn't shared. She refused to allow anyone else to have control over her life. Illness had been her jailer—her parents, her parole officers. She scribbled the word "independence" at the bottom of her list. Katie knew her happiness would come from within. Family was great. Friends were fabulous. But to feel truly independent, she needed to be the helper, not the helped. Wasn't it ironic that the most generous help she had received came from a stranger? It was a gift that allowed her to bury her past and become her future.

"Why me, Bea?"

Her voice echoed off the walls of the empty bakery. It was a question she'd asked herself countless times over the last seven weeks. Why would a woman whom she'd never met give her a bakery in a town she'd never been to?

Katie flipped to the back of her journal, where a piece of worn pink stationery sat tucked close to the binding. The tri-folded paper had been opened and closed hundreds of times. She'd read every line, looking for clues. There was a list of one hundred reasons Bea gave the bakery to Katie, but not one made sense.

You have a good heart, it began, but how did she know? That might have been the biggest clue because it sat at the number one position, but it didn't lead Katie to anything conclusive. *You're a good person* was the second entry. Although Katie tried to give more than she took, she didn't consider herself any more deserving than the next person. She'd logged hundreds of volunteer hours in the pediatric cardiac unit in Dallas, but it never felt like work, and she didn't do it for any reason other than to bring a smile to those around her. Was that what Bea meant when she wrote reason number one?

Katie scrolled down the list:

Joyful to be around.

Pretty smile.

Resilient.

"How do you know?" she asked.

Part of her glowed under the positive accolades. The other part couldn't grasp how this woman knew her. Had Bea stalked her or had her followed? For what purpose? That was the million-dollar question.

Katie looked around the bakery. It wasn't a million-dollar property, but it was something special. Where the pinstriped wallpaper once hung, there was a fresh coat of paint the exact color of soft butter. On the walls were pictures of the muffins she had baked. Photos of the seven daily specials hung in a row.

Behind the counter was the new coffeepot she'd purchased. It wasn't the espresso machine her friend Sage had suggested, but it was better than the percolator that once sat spitting and sputtering on the Formica surface.

No, this place wasn't worth a million dollars. It was worth more because it had changed Katie's life.

In the end, it didn't matter why the older woman had given her the gift. All that mattered was what Katie did with it.

She tucked the pink page back into her notebook, then flipped back to her bucket list and wrote things that came to mind:

Ride a roller coaster.

Meet a celebrity.

Cut down my own Christmas tree.

Fall in love.

Her number one priority was never to overlook an opportunity to try something new.

While Katie continued to jot down notes, she saw a flash of red out of the corner of her eye. Her friend Sage had hopped out of her SUV near Bishop's Brewhouse and headed her way. Her corkscrew red curls bounced with every step.

The bell above the bakery door rang as Sage skipped inside. From her bright smile to her rosy cheeks, she glowed from her happy life with Cannon. Katie couldn't believe only seven weeks ago, Sage had a black eye and an unquenchable desire to flee Aspen Cove, but no one knew better than she did how life could turn on a dime. Good could become bad, and awful could become amazing in the time it took to take a breath.

"What's up?"

Katie rose from her seat to give Sage a hug. At five foot six, she looked like a giant compared to her pint-sized friend.

"Sheriff Cooper's friends are back at the bed and breakfast tomorrow, and the last time they were around, they ate everything but the furniture. Can I take what you have, or do you want to make me two dozen muffins?"

"I'll make them fresh and bring them to the bar tonight." Katie looked at what she had left in the display case. There were just over two dozen muffins remaining. She'd have to whip up another batch for the afternoon crowd anyway. "Is Cannon's brother still coming home tonight?"

"It's a go, as far as I know." Sage plucked a sample off the tray that sat on the glass counter and popped it into her mouth.

"That's great. I hope he follows through this time."

Cannon had been expecting his brother, Bowie for the last two weeks. Bowie had told him twice he was on his way then canceled the day he was due to arrive.

Katie imagined how difficult it would be to come back to the town where both his mother and fiancée had died. According to Doc Parker, it had been a decade since Bowie had been home. Wasn't it time to bury the past like Katie did when she left Dallas?

Sage's bright-green eyes lit up. "Hey, I know cakes aren't your thing ... yet, but maybe you can bake a welcome home cake for Bowie."

When Katie showed up in Aspen Cove, she barely knew how to boil water. Now she made the best muffins in town. They were the *only* muffins in town, but still ...

"I've never made a cake."

Sage cocked her head to the side. "Never? Not even from a mix out of a box?"

"I lived a very sheltered life. Ovens were hot and dangerous."

From the age of thirteen on, Katie had been sickly. Her mother stuck to her like lint on fabric, hovering over her like an aseptic balloon, warding off everything that could set Katie's health back or place her in danger.

"Unbelievable. Even *I've* made a cake. Although I'm most famous for my reheating skills."

"'Famous' isn't the word I'd reach for. That makes it sound pleasant. 'Notorious' is more like it."

Sage laughed as she rounded the corner to get herself a cup of coffee.

Katie had a rule with her friends. If she'd served them a cup at least once, then they were family and could help themselves. However, if a stranger walked behind the display case, she would have nudged them out with a rolling pin. She'd consider a baking pan to the side of the head if they caused her trouble.

"We can't all be Betty Crocker," Sage said.

She followed her friend to the other side of the counter and prepped her new coffeemaker for a cup of decaf. Sage liked her coffee laced with electricity, whereas Katie chose the heart-healthy option of decaffeinated.

Sage looked at the coffee dripping into the cup. "I don't know why you bother drinking that. It's dirty water." She lifted her own octane-filled cup to her lips.

"It makes me feel grown-up without hurting my organs." Katie placed her hand on her chest. Under the cotton, she felt the raised scar tissue from her surgery.

"I'm a nurse, and I don't take care of myself as well as you do."

"You have to take care of the body you've got."

Katie had told no one about her medical history. She'd kept it a secret because she didn't want people hovering over her. For once, she wanted to live her life like everyone else. Her anonymity in Aspen Cove had given her that. What no one knew couldn't hurt her or influence how they perceived or treated her.

"What about the cake? Are you up for the challenge?"

Katie looked over the counter at her journal, which was sitting open on the table. This instance fit the bill as a new opportunity. How hard could making a cake from scratch be?

"I'll do it. What flavor?"

"Let's keep it simple. White cake and white frosting."

"You want frosting, too?" she teased.

Sage shook her head. Katie had seen that incredulous look before on Sage's face. It was the one that screamed, *You're kidding, right?*

"Without frosting, cake is just flavored bread."

"Fine, frosting, too." She pulled her cup from the coffeemaker and took a sip. "What are Ben and Cannon doing today?"

The two women leaned against the counter and looked

7

out the window. What once was a ghost town had new life. It experienced a rebirth every year in May when the tourists and fishermen showed up. The once whitewashed windows of the closed dry goods store across the street were cleaned and now sparkled under the afternoon sun. It turned out that from May to October, the women of Aspen Cove brought their wares to town to sell to the visitors. They offered everything from soy candles to beeswax soap.

"They're at the cemetery. The new grave marker for the Bennett's is being set up today. It has Bill's, Bea's, and Brandy's names carved in granite. Bowie will eventually visit to say goodbye to Brandy, so Cannon wanted it to be perfect."

Katie had been to the gravesite that had only a temporary marker with Bennett painted in block letters. It broke her heart that this little town had lost so much.

"At least Bowie's not coming home to a drunk father," Katie said. Ben had sobered up and stepped back into the roles of father and friend. "He's been a lifesaver here. Without him, I'd be working seven days a week." Katie kept him busy at the bakery. She'd taught him how to make the weekend muffins, which gave her some much-needed time off.

"That's a blessing, for sure." Sage snatched another muffin bite from the sample plate. "I'm not sure how Bowie will acclimate to being back in town. He never wanted to return after Brandy died. He's been tight-lipped about what happened to him in Afghanistan, but he was medically retired from the United States Army, so it can't be good. It's one thing to come back home because he wants to, another if he's back because he has no choice."

"That's so sad, an injury added to a broken heart." Katie imagined both would require recovery time, but she never considered it would take so long to adjust. "You'd think all those years would be plenty of time to get past the grief and move on. Ben did, so I hope his son can, too."

Katie had no earthly idea how long it took to get over losing the love of one's life. She'd never been in love, but she'd added it to her bucket list.

Sage drank the rest of her coffee and tossed the paper cup in the nearby garbage can. "Who knows how long that takes? Everyone works at a different pace."

"Speaking of pace." Katie needed time to figure out how to make a cake. She looked at the muffins in the case. With Ben gone for the day, she was on her own. "You know what? If I'm going to make that cake, I better get to it." She opened the display case and boxed up the remaining muffins. "On second thought, why don't you take these? I think I'll close up early so I can do justice to Bowie's welcome-home cake." The least she could do was provide something sweet for a man, no doubt, filled with bitterness.

Sage gave her a sideways glance. "Are you sure? I've never known you to close early."

"You've known me for seven weeks."

"I think I've got a good handle on you."

What Katie wanted to say was, "You don't know me at all," but she didn't because that would open an entirely different dialogue. She wasn't ready to give up her secrets.

"Sometimes I don't think I know myself." She knew who she wanted to be, but there was a part of her that was a mystery. A part of her that had belonged to another—her heart.

Donors were kept anonymous, so Katie had been in the dark. Records were sealed. She'd thought Bea's daughter's heart might sit in her chest. The April day of her death fell eerily close to Katie's new chance at life, but the rest of the timeline didn't fit. Katie's second chance came years after Brandy's death.

Sage picked up the bakery box and gave Katie a one-armed hug. "The party starts at seven. Everyone will be there."

As soon as Sage left, Katie locked the doors and turned out the lights. There was only one thing left to do. She'd make the best cake she could for Bowie by adding a dash of courage, a pinch of resilience, and the love and compassion she had in her borrowed heart.

CHAPTER TWO

At thirty-four years old, Bowie Bishop didn't think he'd ever come back to live at home. It was never his plan to return to Aspen Cove, but then again, he didn't expect to get shot again while in Afghanistan. When those bullets hit his femur and shattered the bone, everything changed.

He sat at the end of the dock and let his legs hang over the side. The soles of his boots skimmed the water, creating ripples that danced across the smooth surface.

He'd forgotten how high the lake could get after the snow melted; well, not exactly forgotten, more like banished from his memory. He looked across the water to where the tree line split—it was the only place where the side of the mountain dropped off into the lake. He hated that patch of road. In fact, he hated just about everything.

At night, in his dreams, he still saw her—eyes the color of amber, chestnut hair, and a laugh that could warm even the coldest heart. Brandy was his everything, and when he lost her, he knew he'd never be happy again.

The familiar sound of a can popping open and the hiss

of carbonation escaping meant he wasn't alone with his thoughts any longer.

"I thought you might like one before we go to the bar." Cannon sat down next to him and handed over the beer.

"I don't feel much like celebrating my return. I think I'll stay here."

"No can do, bro. You've got a lot of people looking forward to seeing you. If you don't show up, they'll come here. There's no way to avoid it."

Bowie lifted the can to his lips and took several big gulps. It would take a lot more than a can of beer to get him through the night.

"Why did you tell them I was coming back?" This trip wasn't a social visit. It was a place to land until the VA assessed his disability rating, and then he was gone.

"Because seeing you back in town would be like seeing a ghost."

Cannon had described it accurately. He'd been a ghost. Most of him died when Brandy did.

"I don't want the attention."

"Fine, show up, stay awhile. Paste on a fake smile. Then come back here and hide in the house until tomorrow morning, when you get up to run the bait and tackle shop. I've been taking it all on by myself for years. You're back, so you can help."

Bowie never knew his brother to be so stern, but then he figured years of dealing with their drunk father had taken the softness out of him. He'd always felt bad that he left his brother to pick up the pieces, but Bowie couldn't bear to spend another second in the town that reminded him of his loss.

"I'm not staying. Besides, Dad looks like he's got a handle on things. He can run the bait and tackle store."

Cannon had told Bowie how bad his father had gotten, but to look at him now, he couldn't believe it. He knew his brother wasn't one to exaggerate, but Ben looked fine.

"No, he's helping Katie at the bakery. It's where he found his sobriety. It's best if things don't change too drastically for him."

Cannon picked up a few pebbles from the dock and tossed them into the water. Rings formed around the disturbance and spread out wide. That's how life was. One thing created a ripple, and an entire life changed.

"Change isn't good for Dad, but it's okay if *I'm* propelled into a nightmare?"

He pushed the boot of his good leg beneath the surface of the water and kicked forward, sending a splash outward. Ten feet in front of him, a fish leaped from the water to catch a bug.

"It's not my intent to pick at your wounds, but I want a life, too. I gave up everything—my life, my career. I gave it all up to come back here and try to save what we had. When will it be my turn to have something?" He emptied his beer and crushed the can in his fist. "Sage entered my life and changed everything. I'm in love with her, but I need time with her. I won't get that if I'm running two businesses and watching out for Dad."

Cannon was right. Bowie had bailed on his brother, but at the time, he had nothing left to give. As he sat on the dock and looked around, he worried he had even less now than he did then.

"I'm not staying," he repeated.

"I hear you. Just remember, I stepped up when you couldn't. I'm asking you to step up while you're here. I'm rarely selfish, but dammit, Bowie, you owe me."

That was another fact he couldn't deny. He owed

Cannon. He'd given up his dream job to come home and be responsible for the family. He was only twenty-four years old when everything went to hell. Too young to be a full-fledged adult, but too old to be a kid.

"You're right. I owe you more than I could ever repay."

He turned to his left and took a really good look at his brother. He'd grown into a man while Bowie was gone. They'd been close as kids but drifted apart when Bowie fell in love with Brandy. He'd spent all his time with her. The hardest part about losing her was he didn't know how to live without her. He'd made a promise to himself the day they buried her: he'd never allow another woman to enter his heart.

"I'm not asking for blood. I'm only asking you to stay around for a bit. I've missed my brother." Cannon reached over with one arm and bro-hugged him.

"Let's take it a day at a time. Now tell me about this girl of yours."

Footsteps sounded behind them. They turned to see who approached.

Cannon's stoic expression softened, and a smile took over his face. "How about you meet her?"

He stood and walked halfway down the dock to meet the tiny redhead. He picked her up and twirled her around. The only piece of Bowie's heart that remained squeezed so hard it was almost painful. He watched the two kiss.

It wasn't that Bowie hadn't had female companionship since Brandy died. He'd seen plenty of action, but he was always clear about where those relationships would go. Bowie was like a boat full of holes, and you couldn't fill up a leaky vessel. He was a sinking ship and refused to take anyone else down with him.

He struggled to his feet and limped his way down the

dock to meet Sage. She stood in front of him and rose up onto her toes to kiss him on the cheek. It was an odd greeting from a complete stranger, but he liked her forwardness.

"Finally, I get to meet the infamous Bowie."

He looked down at the runt in front of him. "*Infamous,* huh?"

She smiled, and Bowie could see why his brother had fallen so hard. With a smile like that, it was like the sun radiated from her pores.

"Oh, yes. I've heard everything from how you terrorized him as a kid to how you protected him at school."

Cannon looked at her and shook his head. "Sweetheart, that was bedroom talk and should have stayed in the bedroom."

Sage rolled her eyes. "That would mean we couldn't talk about anything. You work so much, I only get to talk to you in bed."

Cannon looked at his brother with a see-I-told-you-so look. Although Bowie knew he'd never fall in love again, there wasn't any reason Cannon shouldn't. Someone in their family deserved to be happy.

"Let's see if we can change that. I'll be around for a bit so Cannon will have more time to spend outside the bedroom."

"Dude, I don't want to reduce my bedroom time; I only want to increase my other time. Who knows, I might want to spend that time in the bedroom, too."

Sage wound up and punched Cannon in the chest. "I'm not invisible here. Don't be talking about our bedroom activities with your brother."

It was hard not to laugh. Here was a woman who, on

her tallest day, reached Cannon's neck, and yet she was in control. God, he missed those days.

"Although due to your height, you're easy to overlook, now that I've seen you punch, you're hard to ignore." Bowie threw his arm around Sage and began the walk to the house. "One thing you should know, none of the Bishops kiss and tell. Your nocturnal secrets are safe. Nothing else is sacred, though, so give me some dirt on my brother. It's been a long time."

Sage told him about Cannon's one-eyed cat. She laughed at the fact that such a tough man could have such a soft spot for a special-needs pet, but she had no place to talk because when they walked into the house, lying at Ben's feet was her three-legged dog, Otis.

"Aren't you the pot calling the kettle black?"

While Bowie walked over to his dad, Sage and Cannon disappeared into the kitchen, saying something about microwaving dinner.

"Hey, Dad. You're looking good." Dad had a nice scar on his forehead from where he fell at the cemetery.

"I'm alive. That's a start." Ben pivoted on the old leather couch to face him. "I was wondering when you'd come in to say hello."

"You could have come outside."

Ben looked down at the beer in Bowie's hand. "I try to stay far away from alcohol."

"Shit, Dad. I'm sorry. I wasn't thinking." Bowie rocked forward to stand, but his dad pulled him back down.

"It's my problem, not yours. I can't expect the world to change because I have an issue with something. I'm learning."

Bowie took his beer and reached over the arm of the

chair to put it out of sight. "You're right, but I don't have to flaunt your weakness in front of your face."

Ben did something unexpected. He leaned in, pulled his son against his body, and hugged him tightly. "I'm glad you're here. I hope you'll stay awhile."

His plans were short-term, but before he could tell his dad, Cannon and Sage called them for dinner.

Just like the old days, Bowie sat in his place at the family dinner table next to the window. While they ate microwaved stroganoff, Cannon and Ben filled him in on all the things that had happened over the years.

Louise Smith had married Bobby Williams, and they recently had their seventh kid. Doc still ran the clinic, although he was older than dirt. Dalton had done time for murder. The town finally got a sheriff, Aiden Cooper, and Mark Bancroft was the deputy. Zachariah Thomas lit himself on fire when one of his stills blew up. While some things had changed, others remained the same. He'd missed having a place where he belonged. He'd missed his family. As much as he hated to admit it, no matter where he ended up, Aspen Cove would always be home.

CHAPTER THREE

Would anyone notice how lopsided the cake was? Katie tried to camouflage the error with extra frosting. Whereas one half of the cake had a mere quarter-inch layer of frosting, the other side had over an inch.

Even after watching a dozen YouTube videos and an episode of *Cake Boss*, it looked like an amateur baked it. In reality, that was exactly what happened. Her consolation was that it tasted good, and hopefully everyone could look past the imperfections and enjoy the cake.

If the party started at seven, then Katie would wait until ten after to show up. That would give enough time for everyone to say hello to Bowie, or so she hoped.

The only reason she was going, she told herself, was Sage had asked her, but she was curious about the man who had left town a decade ago and never returned.

In some ways, they were alike. She'd packed up and left Dallas. Although her departure happened abruptly, she had considered it for years.

There were lots of reasons people ran away, but it always came down to either running from or running to something. In her case, she was racing to have an authentic life. One she couldn't have in Dallas.

Katie looked at the clock; it was time to go. Dressed in blue jeans and a flowered thermal shirt, she entered the chill of the May night and walked across the street to Bishop's Brewhouse. She'd never seen the bar so full, except for the day they buried Bea. It seemed like the town came out for deaths and births. Bowie coming back to town was a sort of rebirth.

Katie knew his presence was important to Ben. She could only imagine what it meant to Cannon. With the sheet cake in her hands, she twisted and turned her body through the crowd until she was at the bar.

Sage stood behind the taps, pulling a pitcher of beer. "You came."

"Did you think I wouldn't? From the sound of the chitchat around town, this man coming home is like the second coming of Christ—a miracle." She set the cake on the worn wooden surface and looked around at the crowd. "I'm a true believer in miracles." Katie never put much faith in anything until the day her heart quit. From that point on, faith was all she had.

"The cake looks amazing." Sage took it and put it on the back counter. "Was it hard?"

"Hard" was a matter of perspective. It was hard to get the courage to try something new, easy to do it once she decided. Hard to take the reality it wasn't perfect, but easy to hide her mistake.

"Not hard at all," she said with a roll of her eyes. "I imagine it's like anything you do the first time—scary but worth it."

She looked to the end of the bar toward the man everyone crowded around. Baking the cake wasn't nearly as hard as what Bowie had experienced. Even though she didn't know him, the telltale signs of stress were written on his handsome face. Hard eyes. Creased brow. The strained twitch from a fake smile. Katie knew all too well the look of being present for everyone else when all you wanted to do was be alone. *Poor Bowie.*

"You want to meet him?"

Sage poured her second pitcher of beer. She looked comfortable behind the bar. Katie was envious that Sage had settled into Aspen Cove so easily, especially when she was the one who didn't want to stay. All this time, Katie had wanted to stay. She'd found lots of things in Aspen Cove she'd been searching for. She'd found friends, a sense of belonging, a purpose. The one thing that remained elusive was love. It was unlikely she'd find it here, where most men were seasonal visitors and the ones who weren't were like brothers or a father. Besides, finding love wasn't her number one priority. Independence took precedence.

"I'll wait. He looks overwhelmed."

She looked back at Bowie, who talked to Cannon. All she could see was his profile. Strong nose. Chiseled jaw. Tan skin. Brown hair. Sitting on a barstool, he was taller than most men who stood around him. His fake smile was heartwarming; she could imagine his real smile would be heart-stopping.

She climbed onto the barstool at the opposite end of the room.

"I'm sure he is." Sage delivered the pitcher to Bowie and Cannon and came back to stand near Katie. "He didn't want to come."

Katie watched the man smile and chat with the town folk. It reminded her of all the visitors she got in the hospital. She'd smile and nod and make nice conversation, but all she wanted was to be alone.

"It's got to be overwhelming."

The crowd split, giving her a chance to get a look at the rest of him. When Sage had said he was medically retired from the service, Katie thought maybe he'd lost a limb, but he appeared fully intact.

A tight, olive-colored T-shirt stretched across his chest, leaving little for her active imagination. His biceps bulged, expanding the band of cotton to its limit. Her eyes followed the line of his body. He was half on and half off the stool. One leg extended, as if ready to bolt at the first opportunity. His jeans, though worn, looked like they were custom made for him. He was perfect all the way from his cropped hair to his black boots. The only thing missing was a Harley. He had that bad-boy look about him. She'd considered him almost too perfect, but then he turned his head toward her, and her heart skipped a beat. A jagged scar ran from his temple to his chin, bisecting his cheek along the way.

Magazine men weren't her thing. Men who sought perfection in themselves often sought it in others, and Katie was far from perfect. She'd learned long ago that the true test of a man was in how he lived with his flaws. Bowie's scar was the sexiest thing about him. He wore it like a badge of honor. She was intrigued to find out how he got it.

"Can I have a soda?" Katie would have loved to imbibe with the rest, but she rarely drank. Given her health condition, it wasn't recommended.

Sage poured her a soda. "Let's give your cake to Bowie."

"You give it to him. I'm happy here."

Sage gave her a growl. "Suit yourself. He's much sweeter than he looks. Then again, wasn't it you who told me you like them to look like murderers?"

Sage picked up the cake and brought it over to Bowie. She said something that made the entire group look Katie's way. She gave them all a weak smile and a wave but stayed put.

Katie liked sitting in the corner, taking everything in. She seldomly had the opportunity to be an observer. A girl could learn a lot about the people of Aspen Cove if she watched long enough. For example, it was obvious which men in town had grown up with Bowie. Mark Bancroft, Bobby Williams, and Dalton Black had that easy look about them. The one that said, "I've got your back." They talked and laughed like they hadn't lost a day together.

The men who hung back, like Sheriff Aiden Cooper and resident lawyer Frank Arden, were taking it all in, just like Katie. Sitting back and observing. In the corner was a group that included Zachariah Thomas and Tilden Cool, who lived up in the mountains and made moonshine. The only reason for their appearance was the free beer.

Then there were the women. Abby, the beekeeper, was too old for Bowie, but it didn't stop her from hanging on to his every word. Lloyd Dawson, a cattle rancher, had come to town with his family in tow. He and his wife, Maggie, had five daughters, ranging in age from eight to twenty-eight. Poor man. It was his oldest daughter, Poppy, who showed the most interest in Bowie. Katie couldn't blame her. Living with her parents at twenty-eight was no fun. Katie figured marriage was Poppy's easiest way out of the house. Her sisters lined the walls like wallflowers, with names like Rose, Lily, Daisy, and Violet. Their only brother, Basil, hung back and drank beer with the sheriff.

Sage waved Katie over. It was a battle lost if Katie thought she'd get away without an introduction. That was until her phone rang. She knew who it was. Few people had her new cell phone number, and ninety percent of them were in the bar, so when she pulled her phone from her pocket, it was no surprise it was her mother.

She pressed answer. "Hey, Mama. Hold on, okay?"

Her mom continued to talk, but Katie pulled the phone away from her ear. She looked at Sage and pointed to her phone, mouthed the word "Mom," and disappeared out the door to take the call. People were overflowing onto the sidewalk, so she rounded the building and walked to the back of the bar.

"Are you there?" her mother asked.

"Yes, I told you to hold on. I had to get somewhere quiet so I could hear you."

"It sounds like a party."

"It's a welcome-home party for a friend's brother." Katie counted to five because she knew it wouldn't take longer than that to get to the next question.

She only got to three when her mom asked, "Where are you?"

"You know I'm not telling. You have the ability to get in touch with me."

"About that, why did you change your phone number? Daddy and I were happy to pay for your service."

Katie inhaled deeply and let the breath out slowly. She'd always considered herself a patient person, but her mom could try a saint on Sunday.

"You were happy to pay for my phone when you could track it. I'm a grown woman, Mama. What's the point in living if I don't have a life?"

This was where her mom would spring a tear. "We only want what's best for you."

Katie heard people behind her, like someone had opened a door to the bar, but the sound muted right away, so she ignored it and replied to her mother, "You want what's safest, but safest isn't always what's best. I had to run away from you and Daddy just to breathe. Mama, I love you, but I can't live if I can't breathe."

"And I can't breathe not knowing if you're okay."

There was no one to see her roll her eyes, but Katie did it anyway. She stood there, staring at the woods behind the bar, and rolled them in every direction she could.

"You're talking to me. I'm okay. In fact, I'm finer than frog hair split seven ways."

"Are you taking your medicine?"

"Yes, ma'am. I'm eating healthy. I'm making friends. I even baked a cake today for the party. I'm happy for the first time in a long time. Please be happy for me." Katie heard a sound behind her and turned to find Bowie tucked into the shadows of the building. He lifted his beer like he was toasting her. She nodded back. "I've got to go. Please trust me to know what's right for me, okay?"

Her mother's exhale was a sign of surrender. Katie would have loved to tell her parents where she'd run off to, but she knew the minute she did, they would be on her doorstep, ready to drag her back to Dallas. She would eventually tell them, but on her terms.

"I love you, sweetheart. I trust you. It's just that I'm as lonely as a pine tree in a parking lot." Katie grew up on southernisms, but her mother never ceased to come up with a new one regularly.

"I'll call soon," Katie told her. She dialed them at least once a week. There was no sense in making them worry, but there was also no sense in talking to them daily. If she did, she might as well move back home.

"Come home soon," her mother replied.

That didn't deserve a response because if Katie said

anything but *I will*, the conversation would go full circle back to the beginning.

"Love you, and tell Daddy I love him, too." She waited for her mom's *I love you, too*, before hanging up.

Katie walked over to where Bowie stood in the darkness. His back leaned against the brick building, one leg anchored to the ground, the other knee bent with the sole of his boot against the wall. The moon glinted off his skin, making it look almost gold and godlike.

"Welcome home, Bowie." She pressed her hand in his direction for a shake. "I'm Katie Middleton."

He smiled.

Help me, Jesus. She was right; there was a difference between his forced smile and the one that came naturally. This smile came from his eyes instead of his lips.

"Nice to meet you, Duchess."

His hand was so large, it wrapped around hers when he shook it. He had hard-working hands. They weren't soft and fleshy like the account managers at the insurance office where she used to work. No, Bowie's hands were calloused and manly and warm and strong.

"Duchess, huh? I can live with that." She liked that he didn't call her "Princess" the way everyone else did. He was the first person to call her "Duchess." "I'm sure you're trying to get some peace and quiet, so I'll let you be."

She turned to walk away, but he stopped her with a question. "You made the cake?"

"I did." She laughed, remembering the condition of the kitchen when she finished. She swore there was more flour on the floor than in the cake. "If it was terrible, just tell me you're a diabetic and couldn't have any. That way, I won't feel awful."

"I liked it … a lot. How did you know I like extra frosting?"

"I'm intuitive, or … I made a lopsided cake and straightened it out with the sweet stuff. You choose."

He gifted her with another heart-heating smile. "I'll go with intuitive." He offered her his beer. "You want a drink?"

Katie didn't want to appear rude. "Thank you."

She took the mug from his hand. It was no longer frosted, but the beer remained cold. She lifted it to her mouth and let the suds touch her upper lip.

"Has Aspen Cove been good to you?" he asked.

His eyes left her and stared out into the blackness of the night. Up in the mountains, it turned dark the minute the sun set. Tonight, the moon was only a sliver and offered no light.

"I love it here. The people are good. It was a true blessing to come here."

"I hear Bea gave you the bakery." He reached for his beer and took a long swallow. "What's your connection to Bea?"

A moment of awkwardness hung in the air between them. They didn't know each other, but they had something in common. They both had a connection to Bea, only Katie's was still a mystery.

"My inner sleuth is still trying to figure it out."

"You will. The one thing I've always known about Bea was she did nothing without a solid reason."

Katie laughed. "She gave me a list of a hundred, but none of them make sense. The only thing I can think of is she found out I did a lot of volunteer hours at a children's hospital."

Bowie kicked off the wall. "That would make sense. Bea loved kids, and she was always quick to reward good behavior." He turned and headed to the bar's back door. "I suppose I should attend my own party. Are you coming, Duchess?"

Katie noticed a slight limp to his walk but ignored it. They entered the bar, where the crowd had diminished. All who were left fell under the categories of close friends and relatives. It made Katie sad that Bowie's father, Ben, had to stay away, but she gave him credit for knowing his limitations.

"Everything all right with your mom?" Sage asked as Katie took the barstool beside her.

"She's still hovering like a true helicopter parent, but hey, she loves me."

"Can't fault her for that." Sage looked down the bar, where the men had congregated. They each had a plate of cake in their hands. Bowie was on his second piece. "Bowie seems to like it. I saw you two walk inside together. Did you get a chance to meet?"

"Briefly. He seems nice."

"He is nice. I'd love it if you two hit it off. Wouldn't that be awesome?"

So awesome, but the timing is wrong. She needed to establish herself first. In the five minutes they'd talked, Katie got a feel for Bowie. She'd always known that when she met *the one*, she'd know it, and something inside her told her he was it. It was more than his looks. His wounds attracted her. She knew what it felt like to hurt—to watch her life slipping away from her and get a second chance to embrace it. Maybe that's what Aspen Cove would be for Bowie. Maybe coming home was his second chance.

"Still on for fishing tomorrow?" When Sage said the word "fishing," she turned up her nose like she could already smell their catch.

"Yes."

Katie bounced with excitement in her seat. Fishing was on her bucket list, and after tomorrow, she'd be able to cross it off. If she were lucky, she'd get *rowing a boat* completed soon, too. She looked at Bowie and wondered if he had a list; if so, would his include silly things like hers? Things like falling in love?

CHAPTER FOUR

The fish flopped onto the dock while Katie hopped around it, making sure the slimy thing didn't touch her.

Sage had been the first one to pull in a catch. She got it off the hook, but it slipped from her fingers and fell to the wooden surface. At first, the two women thought it was dead. Poised over it, they looked at its lifeless body and squealed when the poor thing came out of shock and flopped around their feet.

"Save it," Sage pleaded to Cannon, who stood at the rail and laughed.

"What's the point? You're only going to barbecue it later." He picked the fish up and held it out to her. "If you don't want to eat it, then you should save it."

Sage shuddered before she palmed the fish and brought it to her face. Katie watched from a distance as her friend looked at its mouth open and close. "I'm so sorry, little guppy. Back you go." Sage tossed it into the lake and watched it swim off. "Visit when you get a chance," she called after it.

"Why did you throw it back?" Cannon asked. "The point was to catch it and eat it."

"No," Sage said. "The point was to catch a fish. I've done that. My life is complete."

Cannon pulled Sage into his arms and kissed her. "I'll complete your life."

Katie watched the two interact. A thread of envy wound up her spine and twisted around her heart. Watching them was like watching soul mates connect. There was an energy that crackled under the surface when those two were together. She was so happy her friend had found love and sad she had never experienced anything so wonderful.

"Get a room," came a deep voice from the end of the dock.

Katie turned to find Bowie walking toward them, his limp less noticeable today.

"Don't mind if we do." Cannon looked toward Katie. "She's still zero-for-zero. Care to take over the fishing lesson?"

Bowie scowled at his brother. "I came home for lunch, not to give lessons."

He looked at Katie. His eyes skimmed her body, from her long-sleeved T-shirt to her tennis shoes. She felt a blush rise to her cheeks when his eyes stalled on her bare legs. She'd always considered them her best feature, and now that the sun was out and the temperature in Aspen Cove had risen to about sixty degrees, she was happy to wear shorts and show them off.

"I don't need a babysitter," Katie said. She turned toward the water and prepared to cast her line.

Sage's and Cannon's voices faded as they walked into the house. She didn't need to turn around to see if Bowie was still there; she felt his presence. He was like heat that wrapped around her. She recognized the tightening in her stomach and the uptick in the pace of her heartbeat. Ever since her surgery, certain feelings were heightened. Any kind of excitement or arousal felt ten times more acute. She wasn't sure if it was because her donor heart beat faster than her original heart or because she was more in tune with what her body told her. All she knew was that her attraction to Bowie was undeniable. He fit her type—tall, broad, and brooding. She liked her men damaged. Not that she had much experience with men. With parents more diligent than prison guards, she had never had much interaction with the opposite sex. But with damaged men, her problems didn't seem so problematic. His problems and her problems put them on even ground from the beginning.

Pole gripped in her hand, she ran through the steps Cannon taught her: *Hold the rod at waist level with the reel above the rod. Press your finger to the line, so when you push the doohickey button, the weight doesn't drop to the ground. Pull the rod back and swing it forward, swiftly pointing the tip of the pole at your target. Let your finger off the line so it can fly.*

Katie smiled as the weight hit the water. She let it sink for a count of three and then wound the reel like Cannon had shown her.

Feeling accomplished, she turned around to face Bowie. His hand cupped his mouth to suppress his laughter. His shoulders shook like he was suffering a seizure.

"What?" She narrowed her eyes at him. "That was a perfect cast."

He walked up next to her and gripped the wooden rail of the dock. "You're right. It was a perfect cast."

She turned to face him. At five feet, six inches tall, she

was average height, but Bowie towered over her, which made her feel small. "Why are you laughing?" She tried to sound stern, but it was hard because the smile on Bowie's face made her insides turn to goo. She'd never seen anything so beautiful.

"What are you trying to catch?" He walked around to her other side and leaned against the rail. She wondered if he changed positions so she couldn't see his scar.

"Anything. I'm not leaving until I catch something."

He looked down at her legs, which now had goose bumps rising on her thighs. "You'll catch a cold before you catch a fish."

Little did he know, the gooseflesh was simply a condition of his proximity.

"Sage caught a fish. Why would you think I'm incapable?"

His chuckle came from deep inside him. It moved through his body like a tremor. "I'm pretty sure she used bait."

If there were ever a moment Katie wanted the ground to open and swallow her, it was now. Bowie was right; she'd cast an empty hook.

She turned toward the water and spooled in the line. Swinging in the slight breeze was her barren hook. "I can't believe I did that." It was hard to feel embarrassment for too long because it was so funny. She reached into the open tackle box and pulled out the neon yellow PowerBait.

"That's cheating."

"I don't understand." She set the container on the edge of the rail. "It's what Sage used."

Bowie opened the jar and pulled out a pellet, then held it in front of her. "Using this isn't really fishing." He flicked the glowing ball into the water. "It's like walking naked down the street and not expecting men to look at you."

Katie frowned and leaned against the rail. She didn't understand what he was getting at. "Can you clarify?"

Bowie turned his back to the lake and leaned on the rail next to her. "All I'm saying is, it's not really fishing. There's a skill to fishing. It doesn't really count if you drop the meal in front of the prey and turn on a flashing neon sign that reads 'eat me.'"

"What does it matter if, in the end, I catch a fish?"

"Stay here." Bowie left for a few minutes while Katie looked out at the water. When he returned, he was dangling a worm between his fingers. "Use this."

She took a step back. Katie didn't do bugs or snakes; a worm, in her opinion, was an amalgamation of both. "I'm not touching that."

He stepped forward. "Oh, come on. It's only a worm. If you want to one-up Sage, you'll use it."

"I'm not interested in one-upping Sage. I want to catch a fish."

"Compromise? I'll put it on the hook. You cast the line. You get the bragging rights when you catch your fish."

Katie looked at the neon container sitting on the rail. There was something unnatural to use bait with the texture of a marshmallow and the glow of the sun.

"Fine, but if I don't catch a fish, it's your fault. You'll have to live with denying me the ability to cross this off my bucket list."

"You don't have a very ambitious list." He pierced the worm and watched it dangle from the hook.

She imagined his list, if he had one, would include things like running through fire, hang gliding, or swimming with sharks. There was a dangerous vibe attached to him.

Not that he looked dangerous, but he didn't seem the type to avoid it.

"I want to experience more common things before I try jumping out of an airplane."

She gripped the handle of the pole and went through the motions of a perfect cast. This time when the hook hit the water, she knew she was set up for success. How could she go wrong fishing with the man who ran the bait and tackle shop?

"I've done that hundreds of times. The jump is always exciting. The flight invigorating. The landing terrifying. At least for me."

She reeled in the excess line and waited. "Haven't perfected the landing?" She knew from Cannon that Bowie had been a Ranger. No doubt he had jumped out of many things, including airplanes.

"The landing can be a real bitch when you're dodging bullets."

"I can't imagine, but I thank you for your service. I'm sorry it was cut short by injury." She looked down at his leg. A red scar ran from the bottom of his knee until it disappeared under the frayed edge of his cut-off cargo pants. "Does it cause you a lot of pain?"

"Some, mostly stiffness, but I cope."

"Sometimes coping is all we can do."

Katie understood that concept too well. She'd never experienced a crushing pain as profound as when they cut through her breastplate to remove her heart. It took months to heal. Occasionally, she felt the phantom pains of healing —the sharp stabbing of bones stitching themselves together. It had been years, but some things she never forgot.

A ripple in the water and the bobbing of her line caught her attention. "I've got a bite."

"It's just a nibble. Wait for a second." He stood behind her, wrapped his arms around her body, and showed her how to hold the pole. "On the next nibble, let's give it a firm tug."

His chin sat on her shoulder, and a ripple of awareness coursed through her body. Katie didn't know what made her heart beat faster. Was it that Bowie was pressed against her or that she had a fish on her line?

The end of her pole bent, and with his help, she gave the line a yank. Within seconds, she was in a battle against the fish. By the way the thing fought, she was certain it weighed a hundred pounds. To her surprise, when she finally got it reeled in, it was no bigger than her size eight shoe.

"It's a good size. You want to keep it?" Bowie gripped the slimy fish and finessed the hook from its mouth. The poor thing didn't even get to keep the worm that came out with the hook.

Her head shook before the words were out. "Nope. I'm happy just knowing I caught it." She was so giddy with her accomplishment that as soon as Bowie tossed the fish back into the water, she threw her arms around his neck and kissed his scarred cheek. "Thanks so much for your help."

He stood back and stared at her. "You're easy, Duchess."

"Yes, but I'm told I'm not cheap." She giggled as she took a knee on the dock and packed up the tackle box.

"You're funny, too." He stood above her, throwing a shadow across the dock as she put everything away.

"Only on Saturdays." She closed the container and stood. "I should get back to the bakery so your dad can have lunch, too." She picked up the pole and box and started toward the house.

"How did you get him to work there?" Bowie followed her to the porch, where she dropped off the pole and tackle box, then continued on her way to her SUV.

"That was Sage. She got him started. He only stays because he gets free muffins."

That wasn't the truth. He stayed because, contrary to Katie's desire to be independent, she needed him. One thing she'd learned about Ben was he needed a purpose. Although things might change down the road, Katie provided him with one.

"Will you stay?"

Bowie looked around. His focus landed on the bed and breakfast. "There are just too many memories here for me." He opened her car door. "I'll stay for the summer. Cannon needs the help." His eyes lit on her legs as she climbed into her car.

He's a leg man. "You could make new memories," she said in a hopeful tone. Even though she'd just met Bowie, there was a vulnerability that pulled her to him.

"There's nothing left here for me." He waited for her to put on her seat belt before shutting the door.

She backed out of the driveway. When she turned her car down Main Street, the only thought in her mind was, *I'll prove you wrong.*

She couldn't wait to get home and jot a new item on her list. Somehow, she'd make Bowie see Aspen Cove in a different light.

CHAPTER FIVE

"You want to help in the bar tonight?" Cannon asked. Both brothers were in the kitchen, raiding the refrigerator. Bowie pulled out the rotisserie chicken while Cannon grabbed for the jelly.

"You need help at the bar?" He ripped a leg off the chicken and took a bite. He was a leg man through and through.

"It's Saturday. I could use all the help I can get."

After Katie left, Bowie had grabbed a piece of fruit and returned to the bait and tackle shop. He'd been busy with the influx of tourists. It started in the spring and didn't die down until the first snow.

The smell of baked goods seeped through the walls from the bakery next door. It was a constant reminder of his past. He remembered how the smell of sweets meant Brandy was next door whipping up something delicious. It was a bittersweet reminder to inhale the perfect scent of his past and know she would never be in his future.

Over the years, he'd grown accustomed to the idea that his life would be a string of one-night stands. The best way to avoid a broken heart was not to expose his. Hell, after Brandy died, his heart had dried up and shriveled. It was a wasteland. Many a woman had tried to plant the seed of love in his heart, but it never took hold. Nothing could grow in barren land.

"Let me shower and clean up. I'll meet you there."

Cannon slathered peanut butter on bread and plopped a glob of jelly in the center before he pressed the two halves together. He took a bite. Muffled through the food in his mouth, he asked, "Did Katie catch a fish?"

Bowie smiled at the memory. How proud she looked when he held up the fish. "Yep, she caught a decent-sized trout the right way—with a worm." He tossed the bone from his chicken leg into the trash can. "I can't believe you let her use that crap bait."

That mischievous look took over Cannon's features again. When Cannon's eyes grew wide and that glint lit him up, he was either doing something, hiding something, or guilty of something. Bowie had missed that look.

"I had other plans, and fishing wasn't one of them."

"You really love her, don't you?"

It was a stupid question. Cannon couldn't keep his hands off Sage. When he wasn't with her, he talked about her nonstop. It reminded Bowie of what it felt like to be in love.

Better him than me.

"What do you think about Katie?" Cannon lifted a brow.

"Don't go there. The Duchess seems like a nice enough girl, but I'm not interested."

What he meant was, he wasn't interested in her long term. There was plenty to be interested in for fun. She had legs that would wrap around his waist just right. He couldn't help noticing she was toned and curvy in all the right places. Despite her neck-high T-shirts, it was hard for her to hide her breasts. Breasts Bowie was certain would be the perfect size to fill his large hands.

"It wouldn't hurt you to let someone in."

"Advice coming from the guy who lost less and waited years to do the same. I'll pass."

"Whatever." Cannon grabbed his keys and walked to the door. "Kind of a coward move if you ask me. You're willing to dodge bullets but not risk the razor's edge of a relationship." Cannon walked out.

Bowie couldn't argue with him. Bullets were easy unless they ended a career. He looked down at his knee. The scar started there and ran to his hip. He hated that his brother considered him a coward, but he had no idea how to change Cannon's mind. He wasn't about to fall in love again.

He entered his old bedroom. Nothing had changed; it was like he'd walked out yesterday. On his dresser was his collection of model planes—an obsession since he was a kid. Next to the B-1 Bomber was a ticket stub to a movie he'd seen the week before the accident. He and Brandy went to see *Witch Mountain* because she had a love for all things Disney.

He made his way into the shower and stood under the stream of hot water, trying to wash the memories away. As the water sluiced over his body, he closed his eyes and didn't see Brandy; he saw Katie. He relived the moment when she said she was easy but not cheap.

His body reacted in the only way a man thinking about those long legs wrapped around his waist could. He grew and hardened until he had no choice but to relieve himself. Bowie had done a lot of self-gratification over the years but never had a release held so much power and deliver so much pleasure.

After that experience, he really wanted to crawl into bed and sleep, but his father was home, so he dressed and joined him in the living room.

"Hey, Pops." Bowie took a seat on the sofa next to his dad.

Ben lowered the volume on the television and turned toward his son. "You made it past your first twenty-four hours. I'd say that's the hardest." He reached out and patted Bowie on the shoulder. "It won't be easy, son."

"You're right, but you have to know now, I'm only staying long enough to figure out my next move."

Whatever light Ben held in his eyes dimmed. He lowered his head. "I'm not a great role model for dealing with grief. We all have our own way. Mine was the numbness alcohol provided. I imagine yours is the shot of adrenaline that comes from running for your life." He shook his head. "Neither are healthy options. Mine could have killed my liver. Yours could have flat out killed you. Haven't we had enough death?"

"Yes, we have."

Dad was right. Bowie's life had been surrounded by death that started with his mom and Brandy. Then he joined the United States Army, became a Ranger, and experienced a regular dose of death. He'd become anesthetized to it. Bowie had felt little in years—until her. Something about Katie made him feel. The attraction was palpable, but more than that, something about her got under his skin. He wasn't sure if he liked it or hated it. All he knew was, he had nothing to offer her but a good time. If she was okay with that, then his short stay in Aspen Cove would be tolerable.

"You helping in the bar tonight?" Dad reached for his cup of coffee.

"Unless you need me to stay."

Bowie prayed his dad would ask him to stay, but he knew he wouldn't. The only time he'd known of his father being selfish was every day for the last several years, and he hadn't even seen it firsthand. But the selfish man in him was gone, and back in his place was the father he'd always loved.

"You go help your brother. I wish I could help, but it's not smart to put an alcoholic in a bar. The bakery closes early tomorrow. How about I help you out at the store?"

Bowie laughed. "Still can't believe you're a baker."

"I had to put my energy somewhere else." He patted his stomach. "Can't say eating all those sweets is a better addiction, but at least I'm not waking up in strange places. Besides, that Katie ... she's a special one. Can't put my finger on exactly why, but I think she needs help. Although she'll be the last one to ask for it. What do you think of her?"

"Too early to tell. She seems all right."

He wouldn't tell his dad his thoughts turned carnal each time he saw her. First, that would give him hope there was a chance for Bowie to love again, and that wasn't an option. Second, something told him his father would warn him away if his intentions weren't honorable.

Bowie had no desire to be dishonorable. He'd honor every inch of her body. He'd share every inch of his except for his heart.

"You better get going. There's a crowd in town this weekend. Besides, I'm babysitting tonight."

Bowie's brows lifted. "First a baker, and now a babysitter. I can't believe it."

"It's not what you think. I'm watching Sage's dog, Otis. She should be bringing him over any minute."

As soon as the last word was out, the door opened, and Sage stuck her head in. "Ben, I'm here with Otis. Are you ready?"

Bowie wasn't expecting to get attacked, but as soon as the furry beast cleared the door, he ran directly for the couch. When the dog leaped into the air, Bowie took a good look at his missing hind leg.

So Cannon isn't the only stray she's collected.

He moved his head from side to side, trying to avoid the dog's wet tongue, but it was no use. Otis was intent on giving Bowie a kiss.

"Otis," Sage scolded. "Stop."

The dog looked back at her for a second, then went back to licking Bowie's face. He laughed because no matter how forceful Sage tried to make her voice, she could never instill the feeling of fear in others. The woman was like a tiny leprechaun, red hair and all.

Bowie lifted the dog and placed him in Ben's lap. "You're next." Otis didn't miss a beat. He wasn't particular about whom he loved as long as he licked someone. He looked past the ball of fur to his father. "See you later, Pops."

Outside, he pulled his Harley out of the garage. He'd towed it behind his truck to Aspen Cove and had been dying to ride it. Tonight, the weather was perfect.

"Is that a Harley?" Sage said with a giggle from behind him.

He looked at her with curiosity. He didn't understand what was funny. "You want a ride?"

"Oh, no. You've got the wrong girl. That would be Katie. She loves the bad boys on bikes." Sage walked to her SUV and opened her door while Bowie put on his helmet. "You don't have an arrest record, do you?" She didn't wait for him to respond. She laughed and closed her door.

Bowie had no idea what to think of that conversation. He didn't have a prison record. He might look like a murderer, but he wasn't that guy. He started his bike and throttled it until it growled. He could do bad boy. He could do Katie.

He took the short drive down Main Street and parked in front of the bar. The sun set low in the sky, and within minutes it would hide behind the peak, cloaking the town in darkness. He looked to the bakery's dimly lit windows and wondered what Katie did with her evenings. It wasn't like Aspen Cove was a mecca for entertainment. There was the bar, and that was about it.

He turned from the darkness and entered the light of the brewhouse. His question was answered when he glanced around and saw Katie playing pool with Dalton and his friends. Maybe he was too late to the game. Had Sage dropped a hint?

Staring at the curvaceous blonde, she looked more beauty queen than biker chick. If she liked the bad boys, Dalton wasn't exactly dangerous; he was protective. If the rumors were true, he'd acted more like a protector than a predator when he killed that man. Bowie would have done the same. There were things a man should never tolerate, and abusing women, children, and animals fell into that category.

He walked by the group playing pool, but he knew Duchess's eyes were on him. The heat of her gaze burned through his leather jacket. She may have been physically standing with Dalton, but her sights were on him.

"It's about time," Cannon said. "I was thinking you bailed on me." He nodded down toward the end of the bar where the group of fishermen he'd sold poles to that morning were huddled. "Take their orders and then change the keg to the lager."

Bowie's first instinct was to tell his brother to piss off. He'd never taken orders from Cannon. The brother he remembered wasn't the man who stood in front of him. He'd grown up from a twenty-four-year-old kid into a man.

As soon as the front door opened again, he knew Sage had arrived because Cannon got that goofy, lovestruck look in his eyes. He also knew he'd be watching the bar solo.

As soon as they got the bar stocked, Cannon and Sage disappeared down the hallway to the storage room.

"Can I get a refill?" Katie put her glass on the counter.

"Jack and Coke?" Given the dark liquid at the bottom, it was his best guess.

"Yes, but I'll take mine without the Jack. Never liked that man."

She smiled, and his knees weakened. It was ridiculous how her mere presence had him feeling like a kid. He was far beyond adolescence.

"Coke, it is." He looked past her to Dalton. "You and Dalton a thing?"

Her perfume rose to his nose when she turned to look at the man everyone described as a human oak tree. At six foot four, Bowie was big, but Dalton was even bigger. They grew them large in Aspen Cove.

"Me and Dalton?" She giggled. "No." She shook her head. "He's the older brother I wish I had."

Bowie felt awful for him. Nothing shrank a man's junk faster than a girl who played the brother card. It was as bad as the friend card.

"I heard you liked bad boys." He set her soda on the counter.

She lifted the glass to her lips and took a sip. "I do, but Dalton's no bad boy. He's like Bambi with testosterone. What about you? Are you a bad boy?"

Bowie would like to show her how bad he could be. "I am *the* bad boy."

"Braggart." She turned and walked away.

Cannon showed back up an hour later. For the rest of the night, the brothers pulled beers and poured shots.

No matter where Katie was in the bar, Bowie knew her exact location. He couldn't take his eyes off her. When she got ready to leave, Cannon asked him to walk her home.

"I don't want her walking around the back of the building alone. There are too many strangers in town to risk it."

It was a good argument, but Cannon had seen Bowie watch her all night. He'd commented on it a few times. Bowie knew his brother's intentions were somewhere else.

"Matchmaking is not a hat that looks good on you," Bowie said.

"If I left it up to you, nothing would happen. All talk, no action. Or as they say from Katie's home state of Texas, all hat, no cattle."

"Screw you." Bowie grabbed his jacket and ran out the door after Katie. "Wait up." He reached her in three long strides. "You shouldn't be walking out here alone. It's dangerous."

She looked up and down the deserted street. "I'm not seeing any danger."

They walked around the back to the bakery. When he got her to the door that led to her upstairs apartment, he turned her around, leaned against the wall, and caged her in between his arms.

"Danger is standing right in front of you, Duchess, and

you don't even recognize it." He leaned in and brushed his lips against hers. "I want to kiss you, but you need to know we'll never be more than a good time."

She ran her hands up his chest. "That's all a girl can hope for."

Bowie needed no other encouragement. He pressed his mouth against hers until she opened those beautiful lips and gave him access. When his tongue danced across the velvety softness of hers, a calm blanketed him. If he thought she'd gotten under his skin, the kiss firmly planted her in his system. Each cell he believed dead came to life. Katie Middleton would be a problem for him. Hell, how could she not? She felt like heaven, smelled like flowers, and tasted like trouble.

CHAPTER SIX

The damn man kissed Katie like his life depended on it, and then he walked away. That was Saturday. He'd been missing in action since. Sure, she'd seen him in the bait and tackle shop. She passed by him in the bar, but now it was Wednesday. She hadn't talked to him, much less kissed him again since that night.

It scared the heck out of her that she wanted to do both so badly. Was it because his kisses were superior to any she'd had? Or was it that she felt a connection to him that confirmed what she knew at first glance—he was the one? She felt the tug between them, an invisible string that pulled them together. Although impossible, she knew him somehow, like they were connected by something powerful.

Every time she stood at the bottom of the stairs to her apartment, she closed her eyes and relived that brief but perfect moment.

"We're out of muffins," Ben called from the front.

Katie had been in the back, perfecting her cake-making skills. With the influx of tourists in town, she had to bake a wider variety of goodies. In the corner on a shelf, she'd found several tiny loaf pans. Yesterday, she'd made miniature pound cakes. Today, she was trying out carrot cake.

"I'm on it."

Droplets of sweat built on her brow. With both ovens running and Katie working hard to catch up, she was hot. She opened the back door and returned to dump ingredients for chocolate chip muffins into the mixer.

A shadow fell across the floor. Her eyes followed the elongated gray outline of a body until she reached the man standing in the doorway—Bowie. His hands gripped the doorjamb. He leaned in and pulled back several times. His eyes looked at her and then to the stairs that led to her apartment.

He hid his conflicted look with a smile. "Whatcha making?"

Her heart triple-timed in her chest. It was as if her thinking about him had conjured him. "Chocolate chip muffins."

Although she was super excited to see him, she didn't show it; at least she hoped she didn't show it. Over the last few days, she'd told herself to stay the course. Her desire to be independent had no room for a man who made her heart squeeze with his presence.

"I love them. Are you putting orange in them, too?" He looked around the prep area of the bakery, but he didn't step in.

"You can come in," she said.

He took a tentative step and then backed out the door. "I really can't. It doesn't feel right."

Katie shrugged. "It's okay, I understand. Would you like me to send your dad over with some muffins when they're finished?"

Bowie looked at the ingredients churning in the mixer.

"Only if you put orange in the mix. Bea used to add it, and no one could figure out what made the muffins so special. Brandy once told me orange essence was the secret ingredient."

"I'll try it." When Katie had cleaned out the supplies, she'd found a lot of flavored oils. She had no idea what they were used for, but now she knew.

He stood there and stared at her. There was something else he wanted to say; it showed in his expression, but he kept quiet.

She stopped the mixer and walked over to where he gripped the doorway. "That kiss the other night?"

She knew she was playing with fire. He told her he wasn't looking for anything but a good time. She'd thought long and hard about Bowie's place in her life. He'd made it clear she'd only be a distraction.

He leaned in. "About that." He looked to the ceiling as if the words he needed were printed there.

No matter how much she tried to talk herself out of time with Bowie, she was powerless. She justified her actions by telling herself he'd be the same for her. Bowie Bishop was nothing but a good time. If there was something she needed in her life right now, it was a good time.

"Yes, about the kiss." She lifted to her tiptoes and brushed her lips across his before pulling away. "I'm pretty sure you could do better." One thing she knew was, a man like Bowie wouldn't take kindly to a girl pointing out his faults. Although the kiss he'd given was perfect, it was too short. So ... he could do better.

"Is that right?" He pulled her to him and stepped into the sunshine. "You didn't like my kiss?"

He pushed her against the brick building and pressed his body against hers. His hard chest pushed into her supple breasts. His leg took up real estate between her thighs.

She was good and trapped, but she liked it. "I liked the kiss, but it lacked length." She'd chosen her words with care, knowing he'd read more into it than the kiss.

"Duchess, I can't give you much, but length I've got." He rocked his hips into her.

He definitely isn't lacking length.

She couldn't ignore his repeated warnings. He had nothing to give but his body. That was a lie he told himself, but it wasn't her job to point it out to him. Her only job was to figure out if what he offered was enough.

Could she accept only a part of him—the long, hard part? She'd never had a one-night stand. Maybe that belonged on her list as well. Then again, it was in her nature to give her all. What if she gave him everything, and he gave her nothing but a good time? She'd told him Saturday night a good time was all a girl could hope for, but that was a lie. She wanted more—needed more. She had no right to ask for more. She'd been given so much already, including a second chance at life she refused to waste. She'd learned life was fleeting, and she had to live for the moments.

"I'll take what you've got." Her fingers skimmed up his chest until they wrapped around his neck. Katie pulled him down for a kiss.

"I'll take what you're offering." He took her mouth in a rough, lust-fueled kiss. His mouth was scorching hot against hers. His tongue did a slow sweep along the curve of her lip, making her clench her thighs around his leg.

When he pulled back, his eyes danced with dangerous intent.

"Is the batter ready?" Ben called from the bakery.

Bowie traced her lower lip with his tongue, then nipped

roughly at it with his teeth before turning and heading into the shop next door.

She licked where he'd bitten her and savored the taste of him. It took several gulps of air to get her heart rate to slow down. When she walked back inside, she ran smack dab into Ben, knocking them both off-kilter. She fell to her bottom, whereas Ben was lucky enough to grab the counter for balance.

"I'm so sorry, Katie. I saw the door open and thought I'd check on you." He offered her a hand and pulled her to her feet. "Did you get too hot?"

"Hot" wasn't quite the word for it. She was about two degrees from internal combustion. If Bowie could make her feel like that with a kiss, she couldn't wait to see his other talents.

"Yes, I got a little heated."

"It will only get worse as summer approaches. There's a fan in the storage closet. I'll set it up."

Ben turned and left her to the muffin batter. She searched through the flavor bottles and found the orange. After she added a splash to the mix and blended it in, she scooped batter into muffin cups and put them in the oven. It didn't take long for the smell of oranges to mix with chocolate.

"Is that orange I smell?" Ben walked behind the counter carrying a small fan. He looked through the oven glass and sighed. "You know orange chocolate chip muffins are Bowie's favorite."

Katie smiled. "I had no idea. Chocolate and orange seemed like a logical pairing." Her little fib would never be known. The speed with which Bowie moved as soon as Ben called out made it obvious he wanted no one to know what was happening between them. "When they're done, you can take some to him."

Ben frowned. "Oh, I don't know. It might not be a good idea. Could bring up too many memories." Ben plugged in the fan and watched it oscillate.

Katie stepped in front of the flow of air. She was still overheated, but it had little to do with the temperature in the kitchen.

Twenty minutes later, the timer rang, and Katie pulled out three dozen perfect muffins. People off the street must have smelled them, too, because, within minutes, two dozen of them walked out with happy patrons. She boxed up four and handed them to Ben. "Take these to your son. He'll like them."

Skepticism was written all over Ben's face. "I don't know."

She put the box in his hand and walked him to the door. "Trust me." Katie knew Bowie would like the muffins. He'd told her, but that wasn't something she'd share with Ben.

Ten minutes later, he came back with a smile on his face. "You were right. He loved them. He also said they needed more orange, but what does he know?" Ben reached for a bite from the sample tray and popped it into his mouth. "I think they're fine."

Katie picked up the oven mitt and playfully hit Ben on the shoulder. "We don't serve muffins that are *fine*, Ben. We want them to be *fabulous*. If Bowie says they need more orange, then maybe they do."

"They're good." Ben took another bite and swallowed. "He also said everyone is meeting at Maisey's at five for dinner."

"Is that so? Who is everyone?" A warm feeling oozed through her insides. It was sweet and comforting, like warm syrup on pancakes. Was that Bowie's way of asking her out?

Ben turned off the ovens. It was close to quitting time. "You, Cannon, Sage, Bowie, and me."

"Sounds great."

She condensed what was left in the display case down to a single tray of cookies and the muffins she had left. At the end of the day, whatever didn't sell, she brought to Sage. The poor girl couldn't cook a meal—a real problem because she owned an inn that served breakfast. Thank goodness for leftover muffins and Cannon's Crock-Pot casserole skills. If not for that and the cartons of yogurt she bought, her guests would starve.

"You coming, then?" Ben looked hopeful.

"Is Dalton cooking?"

"No idea. All I know is, it's meatloaf night."

Ben had come so far in such a short time. He no longer drank his sorrow away. He faced it head-on with a cup of coffee and a muffin. "One day at a time" was his mantra, and today was a good day because Ben liked meatloaf.

"I'll be there. Now get out of here and help your son close the bait shop." Katie shuffled him out the door and closed up the bakery.

Mini carrot cakes could wait. She packed up Sage's goodies and raced upstairs to make herself presentable. Any girl worth her salt didn't show up to dinner dressed in jeans and a T-shirt.

She pulled a pink dress from her closet. It was perfect, with its sweetheart neckline and mid-thigh hem. Above the waist, it screamed, *innocence*. Below the waist, it whispered, *ready*.

At her age, she'd had plenty of experience flirting. In fact, she'd get an A in seduction—and an F in everything else. With a hovering mother and a dad who had a collection of guns that could rival Rambo, follow-through was near impossible.

She fluffed her hair, gave a spritz of perfume, and slicked on some lip gloss. Tonight, Bowie wouldn't know what hit him.

She slipped on a pair of wedge heels and walked across the street. She was the last to arrive because it was important to make an entrance. Any respectable girl knew *be there at five* really meant show up tastefully late to attract attention.

By the look on Bowie's face, her plan worked. He wasn't the only one who could dangle the bait.

Up ahead stood Dalton by the swinging kitchen door. He looked at her and smiled. She waved to her group on the way to greet him. He was an important part of her plan. She didn't know Bowie well, but she tasted desperation in his kiss. She felt the strength of his steel rod against her hip. He was ready, but one of the best pieces of advice Katie ever heard was from her Grandma Pearl. She told Katie a girl who showed the good china too early never got to enjoy the tea.

"Hey, Dalton. What are you doing tonight?"

She looked over her shoulder. Sage and Cannon and Ben were deep in conversation. Bowie paid no attention to anyone close to him. His eyes were on her, and she liked the attention.

"Going to the bar."

"Can you skip it tonight?"

Dalton leaned against the counter. "What do you need, sweetheart?"

She leaned in and whispered in his ear, "I need a distraction." She looked over her shoulder at Bowie.

"Thought we could go to Copper Creek. I could use a trip to Target."

He looked past her to Bowie. "Do you know what you're doing?"

She shook her head. "Nope. I'm on the learn-as-you-go plan."

"You know he's broken, right?"

She kissed Dalton on the cheek. "We're all broken."

"I suppose you're right."

She walked to the table and took the only open seat— the one next to Bowie.

"The muffins were great," Bowie said. All eyes at the table went to him the second he spoke.

She scooted in until his jean-clad thighs rubbed against her bare leg. "I'm told they needed more orange."

Bowie gave his father a dark look. "Did you have to tell her I said that?"

Ben shrugged. "I gave up booze. I gave up sleeping on strangers' porches. I gave up lying." He waved Dalton over and ordered five blue-plate specials. "I'm not giving up good food."

As Ben spoke, Bowie slid his hand across her bare knee. No one noticed but Katie. Her entire body responded to the light touch of his calloused finger. The riot of emotions she felt made her heart race. Her body sing. Her core clench.

Dalton returned quickly with the blue-plate specials. It was as easy as plating up what he'd already made. Katie listened to everyone talk about their day. If it weren't for Bowie's hand skimming across her knee throughout the meal, she would have felt like she was at a family dinner with siblings, but no sibling would ever touch her so intimately.

"You ready?" Dalton stood by the edge of the table with his keys in his hand.

"Where are you going?" Bowie asked. "I thought you'd come to the bar tonight."

Katie smiled. She pulled out her lip gloss and touched up her lips. "Dalton and I have plans."

Bowie looked at her like she'd spoken in tongues. "Plans? What plans?"

Katie didn't answer his question. She scooted from the booth, and his hand fell from her knee to the seat. Bowie had been told she and Dalton weren't a thing, but by the look of confusion in his eyes, it appeared he was no longer convinced.

"Katie and I have a date with Copper Creek."

"A date?" Bowie repeated.

Katie put a ten-dollar bill on the table for her share of the meal and gave Ben and Sage a hug before leaning into Dalton and saying, "He goes to great lengths for me." She wrapped her arm around his and walked to the door.

Dalton reached above her to open it and whispered, "Did you see the look he gave me?"

"No, what look?"

"Like he wanted to murder me."

She laughed. Katie had seen the look but pretended she hadn't. There was so much tied up in Bowie's expression. Confusion. Agitation. Loneliness. Jealousy. Bowie Bishop was in phase one of Katie Middleton's plan. She was the hunter, and Bowie was her game.

CHAPTER SEVEN

It wasn't until a hand waved in front of his face that he paid
attention.

"Earth to Bowie. Are you there, man?" Cannon said.

Bowie shook his head and turned his eyes from the door
to where his father, brother, and Sage sat staring at him.

"I'm here." It wasn't where he wanted to be, but he
didn't dare run after Katie. That would give everyone the
wrong impression.

"She looked great tonight, don't you think?" Sage asked.

She had a knowing smile on her face, and Bowie
wondered if it came from intuition or if Katie had told her
about them kissing. Katie didn't seem like the kiss-and-tell
sort of person, but then again, he didn't really know her.

"I didn't notice."

The hell he didn't. That little dress of hers gave all
kinds of mixed messages. With its short skirt, he couldn't
keep his hands from traveling across her skin. Soft skin that
felt like velvet under his fingertips. Though the top of her
dress came nearly to her neck, it hugged what he knew
would be perfect breasts.

"Right," his father said. "Not noticing Katie is like not feeling a nine-point-three earthquake on the Richter scale."

"Seriously, who could notice what she wore when she smelled like oranges and chocolate?"

He took a quick glance out the front door and swallowed his disappointment. He'd been all set to make his move tonight. They could have had a glass of wine or a beer. He'd never seen her drink, so he wasn't sure what she liked. Maybe they would have played pool. He'd even considered a dance or two to whatever played on the jukebox if it got his body pressed closer to hers. Now the only affection he had to look forward to was Sage's three-legged dog or Cannon's one-eyed cat, both of which had taken to him. Whenever Bowie was in the bar with both animals present, they stuck to him like gum to a shoe. He seemed to attract the special ones.

Dalton's mom, Maisey, sauntered over to the table. "You want pie?" Although the question was for everyone at the table, she looked only at Ben. "I made that cherry pie you like so much."

It was an odd feeling sitting in front of his father, watching a woman he'd known all his life get sweet on him. He'd never known his father to be with anyone but his mother. Then again, he'd never known himself to be with anyone but Brandy.

He sat back and watched the two talk about pie and adding ice cream to make it sweeter. There was something comforting about seeing his father move on. He didn't want him to remain single and lonely for the rest of his life. Ben deserved to find joy and love after all these years.

Bowie glanced at his brother with Sage. It was also good to see Cannon find love. Feeling like a fifth wheel, he pulled cash from his wallet and set it on top of Katie's ten-dollar bill.

"I've got inventory to take care of. I'll stop by the bar later."

Bowie left the diner and walked back to the bait and tackle shop. When he was a teen, he volunteered to run the shop because it was located next to the bakery, where the cookies and muffins weren't the only tasty things. Back then, he and Brandy would steal kisses behind the store, much like the kisses he coaxed from Katie.

Times had changed. Life had hardened his heart, wounded his soul, and scarred his body. It struck him as funny to realize that once again, there was something sweeter than baked goods at B's Bakery. Maybe things hadn't changed so much after all.

Katie Middleton had cast her line. This time it was baited with her enticing smile, soft lips, and kisses that made him crave her deliciousness. She'd reeled him in. For almost a decade, he'd avoided being caught, but something told him he wouldn't mind so much taking a bite at Katie. He knew he'd never be hooked for good. Even if he wanted to be, he didn't deserve someone as sweet and kind as the little blonde next door. Eventually, she'd see him for the man he was—a man incapable of much more than a few hours of fun. She'd eventually cut him loose, but until then ...

He was halfway finished with inventorying the bait when his phone rang. The screen flashed with the name "Trigger."

"Trig. Where are you?"

Bowie had served two tours in Afghanistan with Trig Whatley. He left the service a year ago. The same IED that sent shrapnel slicing through Bowie's gut had completely removed Trig's leg. It had been a long recovery for his friend, but they'd stayed in touch.

"I heard you got out. You could have come to California, where the weather's warm and the girls wear Band-Aids and string to the beach."

The only people who knew Bowie had been released were the men from his unit and his family. It wasn't something he broadcasted around. The shame of being considered unfit for duty chewed at his insides and ate up his self-esteem. If he wasn't good enough to be dropped in the desert, what was he good for?

"I came back home for a visit. Haven't seen my father or brother in years."

"You staying there?"

Bowie looked around the bait shop. The inside resembled a cabin, with its knotty pine paneling, and stuffed fish hanging from plaques on one wall. He still held the record for the biggest lake trout, which hung in the center of the smaller trophies.

"Nope. Just hanging out for a bit."

"Any hot chicks?"

He thought about the town and the female population. There were quite a few single women in town, most of whom he'd known in high school, but when Trig asked about hot chicks, only one came to mind. That was Katie. Blonde hair. Blue eyes. Nice rack. Small waist. Perfect heart-shaped ass.

"No, man. There's nothing worth getting excited about over here in Aspen Cove. No Band-Aids or string bikinis." There was Katie, but he wanted to keep her his little secret. Besides, he wasn't sure how he felt about her, but he wasn't interested in sharing.

"That sucks. Have you heard about Sledge?"

Bowie laughed. Sledge had been the newest guy in the platoon. Got his nickname from hammering every girl he could talk into his tent.

"No. What about him?" He hoped he didn't fall by way of injury, like himself and Trig.

"He knocked someone up, and now he's a baby daddy, but the kicker is, she had the baby, handed it over to him, and then left. He's asses to elbows in diapers and formula."

"You're shitting me!" Bowie took a seat on the stool behind the counter. He dumped out a collection of flies that needed sorting. "Sledge is raising a kid?"

"Sure as shit, man. No help either. He blames it on the sand."

"Blames what on the sand?"

"The pregnancy."

What an idiot. "We both know sand mixed with an egg doesn't produce a kid."

"True enough. That's not it. He says the heat mixed with the constant blowing sand undermined the effectiveness of his condom supply. Something about the foil packages getting blasted in the field."

Bowie continued to separate the flies by type. "I used plenty of condoms in the field and never had a failure."

"She's a beautiful little girl. Named her Sandra."

Bowie shook his head. "Perfect. And I bet he'll call her Sandy as a reminder of his lame excuse." He pulled out the plastic bin that held the flies and put the sorted ones in their corresponding sections. "What about you? How's the leg?"

"Gone," Trig said with his deadpan demeanor.

"No shit, Sherlock. I'm the one who tied the tourniquet."

Bowie would never forget that day. It was on his list of

the two worst days of his life. The first being the day Brandy and his mom died. The second being that day when the Humvee was cut in half by an IED. He'd been in the front passenger seat. Trig had been in the back. Two of their squad died that day. While Bowie's gut bled like a fountain, he'd been more concerned with keeping Trig tied to Earth. Field training had him acting fast. He'd stopped the flow of blood before his buddy was emptied out, then took care of himself and waited for the medic, who was several hundred feet away in their caravan.

"Thank you for that. I wouldn't be here without you." There was a long pause. "As it turns out, I've got a slick new leg. Two, actually. One that looks more or less like my old leg down to the hair, and I've got a blade runner."

"Are you running again?" Trig had been the fitness king of the platoon. He was always on the go. When he lost his leg, Bowie wasn't sure if the man would recover. When you lose a limb, everything changes. He knew that to be certain.

"I am. I'm thinking about giving the Rock 'n' Roll Marathon a go this year."

"Damn, that's awesome." He'd seen a lot of soldiers bounce back from horrific injuries. In fact, the men who suffered physical injury fared better than those with emotional scarring. Bowie had both.

Although Brandy wasn't one of his appendages, she was a part of him. They had been connected at the hip their whole lives, so when she was gone, he felt incomplete. How did he move on from someone he loved so much? The memory of her remained chained around his heart. Losing her love pulled at him so tightly, he couldn't breathe at times. How could he pretend that love hadn't existed? It was near impossible, but he tried.

"What about you? Are you healing?"

That was a tough question. He would recover from his physical injuries, but his leg would always act up, and his joints would hurt. By the time he was fifty, who knew what his back would be like? But he was certain Trig wasn't talking about those. He had been the only one Bowie had confided to about his losses.

"I'm still here." It wasn't saying much, but it was all he could say.

"That's something, for sure. One thing I learned when my life was hanging in the balance was there weren't an infinite number of minutes. Use yours wisely, my friend."

They said their goodbyes, and Bowie sat in the silence of the closed shop. He pulled out the faded picture of Brandy and wondered what she'd look like today. Where would their life have taken them? She wanted to stay in Aspen Cove, close to her mother and the people she had chosen as a family since hers had been so small. Bowie had wanted to explore the world. Now that he'd done that, he'd come back to the place they'd both called home, but it had changed. He had changed. Everything had changed. But somehow, it was still home. He hated it and loved it all the same. There was comfort in knowing a person could leave for years and never truly be forgotten.

Rather than tuck the picture back into his wallet, he pinned it to the corkboard that had been hanging in the shop since he could remember. At the top it read, "All Stars." That seemed the perfect place to memorialize Brandy. He knew he had to let her go. Trig was right. There were only so many minutes gifted to a lifetime. What would he do with his?

Once the inventory was complete, he stood by the door

and looked over his shoulder at the picture of Brandy tacked to the wall. She would have loved more minutes in her life. She would have traded anything for them, and here he was wasting his. That had to change. He flipped off the lights and walked out—tomorrow was a new day.

CHAPTER EIGHT

Katie supposed she could have asked Bowie to go rowing with her. It was another item she wanted to mark off her list. Fishing—check. Rowing—almost check. Roller blading—next. She had a list of low-risk activities she'd never tried. The problem was, doing them by herself wasn't much fun. New experiences were better shared.

Now that Sage was with Cannon, they spent a lot of their time doing couples' stuff. On the off chance Sage wasn't with Cannon, she was at the clinic or taking care of her bed and breakfast guests. Much of the time, Katie was on her own.

The smell of muffins lifted through the floorboards. Ben was busy baking for the Sunday crowd. Who would have thought taking him in as a favor to Sage would turn him into the best employee she ever had? The only employee she ever had, but he was still top-notch.

It was banana nut muffin day. Maybe she'd box up a few and bring them to Bowie. He was open until noon. That was part of the problem with small-town businesses. They were too small to hire people and too dependent on the seasonal business to close down, so most of the business owners worked seven days a week. At least she had Ben.

Bowie had been hanging around for the last two days. He'd stick his head in the bakery and say hello, but he wouldn't step inside. She understood how painful that might be. The bakery had to remind him of his loss.

She stayed clear of the alley behind the shops. Not because she didn't want his kisses; she wanted to kiss him more than anything, but she wrestled with her desire for Bowie. She wanted him, but would her desire make her dependent on him? Could she have him and not need him? She'd go after Bowie on her terms.

The trick was to get him to want her. Need her. Her decision on how to proceed was based on the laws of supply and demand. If her kisses were rare, then they would be sought. Who wanted a kiss they could get anytime they pleased?

With her mind made up, she dressed to attract in cut-off shorts she paired with a white tee and plaid shirt tied around her waist. On her feet were her favorite red cowboy boots. You could take the girl out of Texas, but you couldn't take Texas out of the girl. She pulled her hair into a high ponytail and slicked on some pink gloss before she headed downstairs.

"Hey, Ben."

She walked over to him and gave him a smooch on the cheek. A month ago, she thought he was close to seventy. He'd been gaunt and sickly looking with yellowed skin. Now that he'd plumped up, his skin pinked, and his eyes held a healthy glow, he looked more like his fifty-two years.

"Good morning, Katie. How did you sleep?"

"Like a baby."

She slept well. Her cardiologist worried about the high

altitude affecting her, but it hadn't. The opposite was true. She found the crisp mountain air invigorating. To Katie, it was a calculated risk. She traded the smog and pollution for clean air and less oxygen. Over the years, she'd learned to listen to her body—she ate well, exercised, and got plenty of rest.

Ben pulled a tray of muffins out of the oven and set them on the counter. "I've got an order for two dozen from Sage. I'm sure a dozen are for her and the rest for the guys coming in later this afternoon. She's got a houseful of city slickers arriving soon. Pretty boys from Denver who think they can fish."

"Pretty boys, huh?" She picked up a four-pack box and gently placed the warm muffins inside. "I'm not much for pretty boys, but it will be nice to have some new faces in town."

"It's a madhouse out there today." Where no cars were parked last month was now a full lot.

They both looked out the window at a full and bustling Main Street. Katie thought it was a beautiful day: The sun was out. The sky was blue. A perfect day to be on the water.

"What are you doing today?" Ben asked.

"Rowing this afternoon."

She watched a woman lead her smiling child into the candy shop across the street. A resident of Gold Gulch set up the sweet shop where the tailor's had once been. It was funny how sweet Aspen Cove had become with the bakery and candy shop and Maisey's pies. Katie loved to watch the eyes of a child when they saw the lollipop as big as a dinner plate in the window or the taffy pulling machine working all day long making saltwater taffy in a rainbow of colors.

"But first I'm delivering muffins to your son, and then I'm going shopping. I saw Abby bringing in a box of goodies last night. I'm certain something in it was meant for me." The reality was, Katie rarely bought anything for herself. Most of the trinkets she purchased, she sent to her family and friends.

The dry goods store across the street was one of her favorite stops. New things got delivered every day. Yesterday, she bought deer jerky. She couldn't say she was a fan, but she got to cross *eat wild game* off her list, and Ben finished it, so nothing got wasted.

Anything Abby Garrett made with her honey was a favorite—especially the soaps and lotions that seemed to turn Katie's dry skin into silk.

Even Cannon had a few things in the country store. He'd started whittling again. Although Christmas was far away, the ornaments he carved were sold as fast as he made them. Katie would never tell him she was the one who bought them up like they were underpriced diamonds. They were her guilty pleasure. She hoped he carved enough of them to fill her Christmas tree. She loved the animals the best, but the Santas and angels were nice, too.

Katie turned to Ben. "Close up at noon. You need time off, too."

"Thanks, Boss." It was funny to have Ben call her "Boss," but she supposed the weekly paycheck she'd given him made it true. "I've got a date with Maisey tonight."

Katie almost dropped the muffin box. "Maisey?" She didn't see that one coming. "That's great. Where are you two going?"

Ben smiled. "We're going to Copper Creek to watch that new Liam Neeson movie."

"Ooh, I hear it's a real nail-biter. Have fun, Ben."

She left the bakery with pep in her step. Miracles happened every day around her, and for the first time in a long time, she was happy. She could only be happier if a grumpy ex-soldier decided she was worth more than a good time.

She entered Bishop's Bait and Tackle for the first time ever. It reminded her of a miniature Bass Pro Shops. The only thing missing was a jumbo fish tank and a bunch of taxidermy wildlife.

She figured it would smell like salmon eggs or the dirt the night crawlers lived in, but it didn't. It smelled like Bowie, which was a combination of amber and pine and pure male.

"Duchess," he said in that slow, lazy way he'd perfected. The sound left a tingle tripping down her spine, as if Bowie had slid his tongue from that sensitive part of her neck all the way to her earlobe. "What brings you in here? Going fishing again?"

She stood about ten feet from the counter and lifted the muffin box like it was a sacrificial offering. "No. I came bearing gifts—banana nut muffins."

He leaned forward and smelled the air. "All I smell is you."

She shifted her head to the side. "What do I smell like?"

"Trouble." He patted the counter in front of him. "Come closer. I won't bite, and if I do ... you'll like it."

That kind of talk made her knees buckle. She liked a man who was confident enough to say what was on his mind. She'd like him better if he could deliver on his words.

"I've been bitten by you." She thought about the day he bit her lower lip. "I liked it." She approached the counter and set the muffins on the glass case that held the most expensive reels.

"Is that right?" He leaned forward until their mouths were a whisper apart. "You must not have liked it too much since you've avoided a repeat." He was so close that when his tongue swept across his lips, it touched hers, too.

She flicked her tongue out to taste peppermint. He smelled like sex appeal and tasted like mint. "I've been busy."

"How was Target?" Inside, she laughed because although he asked about Target, he really wanted to know about Dalton.

"Good. I picked up more orange essence."

"You went to Target for that? I'm pretty sure they have it at the corner store. If not, Marge from the corner store could order it for you."

She opened the box. The smell of bananas lifted from the warm muffins. "You said the chocolate chip muffins needed more orange." She pulled one of them free and separated the top from the base. Breaking a small bite off, she lifted it to his mouth. "Why don't you tell me what's right or wrong with this one." She brushed the bread against his lip, but when he opened his mouth, he didn't only take in the treat; he pulled in her finger as well. If she weren't already leaning on the counter, she would have puddled into a heap on the floor.

He pulled her finger from his mouth but didn't let it go. When he swallowed the bite of muffin, he licked the crumbs from her wet finger. "Delicious."

Katie didn't know if he was talking about the muffin or her. "Your dad made them."

Bowie chuckled. "Oh, you thought I was referring to the muffin. That tasted fine, but you taste better." As quick as lightning, his hand wrapped around her neck and pulled her to him. He whispered against her lips, "Can I taste you, Duchess?" It wasn't a question because his mouth covered hers before she could answer. They were doing a thorough taste test of each other when the bell above the door rang, and a group of men walked in. Katie pulled away, and Bowie gave a low, throaty growl.

"Stick around," Bowie said. "We're not even close to finished." He walked around the counter to the men who stood under the mounted jumbo-sized fish. "Can I help you?"

Katie moved to the side and watched the three men who stood next to Bowie. No doubt they were trust fund babies. Probably the pretty boys from Denver Ben mentioned. Each one was at least a head shorter than him. They were dressed in polo shirts, khaki shorts, and boat shoes, while Bowie wore a threadbare cotton T-shirt and a pair of jeans. On his feet were heavy black boots. Despite his dressed-down appearance, he was a hundred times sexier than the playboys.

Whereas the trio's hair was precision cut, their brows waxed, and their skin spa nourished, Bowie had a rugged look about him. One that said he didn't need an eighty-dollar haircut to make him a man.

One man pointed to the big trophy fish in the center of the wall. "That fish come out of the lake?"

Bowie nodded. "Caught it myself ten years ago. Took me two hours to pull it in." The sound of pride lifted his voice.

"Give me what I need to catch something like that."

Bowie turned to Katie and shook his head. Even she knew it wasn't wise to enter a shop and give the guy behind the counter carte blanche when it came to picking out your purchases.

His two friends chimed in and asked for the same.

Katie would enjoy this. Bowie would either give them what they needed or what they asked for—two very different things. The next few minutes would tell Katie a lot about Bowie. Was he an honest man? Part of her wanted him to be a stand-up guy. The other part of her wanted him to be a big fat liar, because if he lied, then there might be a chance for more, despite his warnings.

Bowie moved around the shop like he'd worked there his entire life; then again, prior to his exodus, he probably did.

Fifteen minutes later, Katie was squeezed into the corner while the three men paid for their rods and reels and worms.

"Anything else you need?" Bowie asked as he rang up their supplies.

To Katie's surprise, he hadn't taken them to the cleaners. He'd even talked them out of expensive, unnecessary equipment.

The blond turned and pointed at Katie. "I'll take one of those." He moved forward and offered his hand to introduce himself.

"Don't touch what's not yours." Bowie's voice became dark and direct.

The brown-haired man next to the blond grinned. "Are you his, doll?"

Katie placed her hands on the blond man's chest and pushed. "I'm not anyone's." Her voice held no fear, but inside, her stomach twisted into knots.

"Not yet." The cocky man leaned in. "We've got time."

She marched past him and walked behind the counter to stand behind Bowie. Her mom always told her when danger came at her to hide behind a solid structure. She was pretty sure it was referenced to a natural disaster when she made that statement, but Bowie was built like a cement wall. He'd work well as a solid structure in this case.

"You can leave in one piece, or I can reduce you to chum and bait. Your choice." Bowie pushed the bag of equipment into the blond's chest. His solid structure grew before her eyes—his stance got wider, and his chest got broader. The surrounding air seemed charged with danger. "Leave."

Her hands ran across the broad scope of his back, tracing the hills and valleys of a body built for war. Under her fingertips, the stone-hard muscles softened.

As soon as the three men walked out of the shop, Bowie turned to face her. Desperation and need filled his eyes. He pushed her back against the wall and looked deep into hers.

"Now, Duchess, where were we?"

CHAPTER NINE

Lush. That was the only way to describe her body. Pressed up against her, she was soft in all the right places. Oh ... and the way she smelled so sweet was comforting. Cinnamon and sugar. Like walking inside the house on a winter's day and smelling freshly baked cookies. Somehow, what Katie baked soaked into her pores. Even her kisses tasted like treats.

The way she kissed him left no doubt she was as hungry for him as he was for her. A few nibbles at her lips weren't enough. He wanted to consume her. Thinking about her was so much easier than thinking about everything he'd lost in this town.

"I'm going to kiss you until you're drunk on me." He covered her mouth with his and savored her sweetness. The kiss began soft and gentle, but something needy and primal took over.

She gripped the front of his shirt, pulling him closer.

His tongue ran along her lips, coaxing them open. He was certain if he could have a taste of her, he'd feel less empty. Being in Aspen Cove had hollowed him out. The only way to survive was to fill the void with Katie.

She shifted her body. For a second, Bowie thought she'd break the kiss and move aside, but that wasn't her intent. He'd pushed her against the All-Stars board. She'd adjusted herself and in doing so, he'd moved enough that Brandy's picture smiled back at him.

"Shit." He broke the kiss and stepped back. "I'm sorry." In his mind, he wasn't sure if he apologized to Brandy or Katie.

Her eyes followed his to the wallet-sized picture. "Oh ... is that her?"

He didn't need to explain; she intuitively knew. "Yes, I'm sorry. It's not right."

Katie licked her lips. "Tasted right. Felt right." She looked at him. "Someday, Bowie, you will learn to live again." She raised her hand and touched the picture of Brandy. "I didn't know her, but my heart tells me she'd want you to be happy."

"It's hard knowing she'll never get the chance to be happy here again." He took a few steps in reverse until his back hit the glass counter. "Have you ever been in love?"

Katie's smile lit the room. Even the dark wood paneling appeared lighter. "No, but I plan to give it a try. It's on my list."

He laughed. Her list was unconventional. "You can't plan love; it just happens. Sometimes it's gradual, like it was with Brandy and me."

He turned and walked around the glass case, putting a barrier between them. Lord knew, when he got close to Katie, all he wanted to do was touch her and kiss her, but he didn't want Brandy looking on. It felt wrong, like he was being unfaithful.

She tugged to tighten her ponytail. "Sometimes you know the minute you meet someone that they're the one ... or so I've heard." She took another look at the picture. "She was beautiful."

"Inside and out." He picked up the glass cleaner and sprayed the counter. At least cleaning kept his hands busy. "You should be careful around those guys while they're in town. I didn't like the way they were looking at you like you were some kind of morsel to eat."

Her laugh was as sweet as her smile. "Oh, you mean you didn't like that they looked at me in the same way you do." She lifted the muffin box, so it didn't get hit with the cleaner.

"I'm different." The words made sense in his head but sounded ridiculous when he spoke them.

Once he'd dried the counter, she put the muffin box back. "What makes you different?"

"They'll take what they want and leave."

"So will you." She pulled out her phone and glanced at the screen. "I've got to go."

Something about her expression made everything tighten inside his chest. He was a hypocrite and knew it. Each time he'd kissed her, he'd told her it meant nothing, but his need to be near her sure meant something. It was something he wasn't ready to admit to himself.

"Where are you off to?"

She pulled out a journal from her bag. "Bucket list. Today, I'm rowing a boat."

Something about that made Bowie laugh. Not the chuckle kind of laugh, but the kind that made his belly ache. "You're going to row a boat? That's like me saying I'm going to get a pedicure."

She lifted her shoulders and stood tall. "Not the same at

all. I'll look good in a boat. You'd look silly in Sex on Fire nail polish."

"Can't argue with that."

Once, in high school, Brandy had painted one of his fingernails pink. It wasn't a good look for him. He'd forgotten about it until someone pointed it out. He had to beat two kids down to reestablish his manhood and stop the teasing.

"Where are you getting a boat?"

"Seth O'Grady is saving me one."

"O'Grady's is overpriced. Besides, Seth is a perv." That was his memory anyway. When they were kids, Seth hid under the bleachers to look up girls' skirts. Although he hadn't seen the guy in years, that was how he'd always remember him. "I'm not sure you'd be safe around him."

She closed her eyes and sighed. "Too late, I've already reserved the boat. If you're worried about me, maybe you should come along."

"Maybe I should." He told himself he'd go to make sure she was all right, but he lied. He simply wanted to bask in the warmth of her presence.

"It's a non-date, then." She spun around and walked to the door. "You want to drive, or do you want me to drive?"

He followed the line of her body, from the top of her ponytail to her red boots. "I'll give you a ride you won't forget." That sentence could be interpreted in so many ways. Bowie didn't care how she took it. He'd deliver regardless.

"I'll be outside at noon ... waiting." She walked out the door.

He watched that heart-shaped ass of hers sway back and forth as she crossed the street and disappeared into the dry goods store.

What the hell am I going to do with her?

He looked at the photo of Brandy. For the first time in years, he heard her voice in his head.

Be happy, she said.

BOWIE CLOSED up the shop and raced home to change. He didn't do board shorts and boat shoes like most of the tourists. Hell no, he wore cut-off camouflage BDUs and biker boots. Those who didn't like it could piss off. He wasn't posing for *GQ* magazine.

His stomach growled. He was hungry. Had Katie eaten? She'd brought him muffins, which he'd finished in short order. The least he could do was bring her lunch. Sadly, the options were limited to peanut butter and jelly or bologna sandwiches. He made one of each and snatched two bottles of water from the refrigerator before he left the house.

He tucked the provisions in his saddlebag and hopped on his bike. He'd promised her a ride she'd never forget, and he'd start with the bike.

The throaty growl of the engine was a sexy sound and came second only to a woman screaming *yes, yes, yes.* He put on his helmet and took off toward town.

Katie grabbed a piece of shade near the bakery. Gone were her boots, and in their place were white tennis shoes. Not as sexy as the red boots, but with those long legs, she'd be gorgeous in anything.

She looked at her phone and glanced down the road. She was looking for him.

He pulled up in front of her and revved the engine before he pulled off his helmet. He thought she'd smiled widely before, but her normal smile was nothing compared to the grin that nearly split her pretty face. The woman hopped up and down like she'd won the lottery.

"You've got to be kidding me. This is yours?" She ran to where he sat and extended her hand to touch the black gas tank. His Harley was solid black, with hints of chrome. She skimmed her fingertips around him and his bike as she made a full circle. "You're perfect."

He killed the engine. "Only if you like damaged goods." He took her bag and put it in the other saddlebag.

"That's my type. Tormented and twisted."

"Good to know." He unhooked the spare helmet he had strapped to the back and placed it over her head. "Have you ever ridden?"

"No."

"Another thing to check off your list." He pushed the helmet down on her head, and she winced. Her hair was in the way of it fitting properly. "Sorry." He removed it and pulled the tie from her ponytail. Long and blonde, her hair fell over her shoulders. The scent of her shampoo lifted in the air. "Strawberry?" He leaned in and breathed deeply.

"Yes, Abby makes it. She makes the best stuff for hair and body." She took the helmet out of his hands and placed it back on her head. "Is this right?"

He pulled the strap tight, then climbed back on the bike. "Hop on, Duchess. Hold me tight. I don't want you falling off."

When she climbed on, she scooted in close, pressing her breasts against his back. He was cradled between her thighs, and it felt nice—more than nice.

He pulled onto the road and gunned it while she held on tight, her whole body glued to his. That was nice, too.

Twenty minutes later, he drove into the parking lot of O'Grady's Equipment Rentals, which sat on the east side of the lake. In the summer, they rented everything from kayaks to fishing poles. In winter, it was snowshoes and snow-mobiles.

Bowie parked and helped Katie off the bike.

"That was the best," she said in a Christmas morning voice.

Her cheeks were pink from the wind. When he pulled the helmet from her head, it gave that just-got-laid look to her hair. Or at least that's what he imagined she'd look like after they slept together—all pink and flushed and sexy.

An uncomfortable ache in his groin told him to keep his thoughts on simpler things like lunch and boating. "You ready to row?"

She took her purse from Bowie and looked down at the bike. "I want to do that again."

Adorable was the only way to describe her exuberance. "You'll have to unless you want to walk home."

"Can we take the long way home?"

Bowie wasn't sure he was ready to drive the circle around the lake yet. "Let's see how you feel after an after-noon of rowing." He grabbed the sandwiches and water. "I brought lunch. You have a choice of peanut butter and jelly or bologna. What's your poison?"

"Is that bologna with mayo or mustard?"

He gave her an incredulous look. The kind that said, *duh.* "Mustard is the only way to go."

"Can we share both?"

He gave her an exaggerated eye roll. "You want every-thing." It was easy being with Katie. She had a go-with-the-flow personality.

"I'll take what I can get with you."

Was that a message? Was she willing to settle for so little? "You should set your standards higher."

She hugged his arm and walked him toward the entrance. "'Low standards' aren't words that come to mind when I think of you."

"What comes to mind?"

He pulled the door open, and she walked in front of him. God, he loved those shorts. They ended just at the curve of her ass. Nothing showed, but hell, his imagination ran away with what was under that frayed edge.

"Tempting." She walked at a quicker pace to the register where Seth stood smiling at her.

"Katie, right?" The man took too much time looking her over.

"And me," Bowie said in a less than friendly voice. The tension strung wire tight through his body. He walked up behind Katie and rested his chin on the top of her head and relaxed.

Seth appeared to take in the situation. "Didn't you just get back?"

Bowie narrowed his eyes at him and Katie. He hoped it looked like a sign of possession. Katie didn't belong to him, but Seth didn't know that. The one thing he'd make sure of was Katie would never belong to Seth. She was far too good for that scumbag.

"Not too long ago." He placed his hands on Katie's hips and tugged her back against his front. She leaned against him like it was a natural move.

"You work fast." Seth handed the bill to Katie. "It's fourteen an hour or thirty for the day."

Bowie pulled out a ten and a twenty and set them on the counter. "We'll take it for the day."

Katie twisted her head to look up at him. He knew an argument was coming, so he kissed her into silence. "Ready?"

Seth pointed to the front door. "Grab the oars on your way out. The boat is in slip number three."

Bowie turned Katie around and guided her out the door.

"Caveman much?" She walked next to him. "What was that all about?"

"I don't like him. I don't like the way he looked at you. Like he had a chance. He's not good for you."

"I didn't realize when I invited you along, I'd get dating advice. What else does this package contain?" She lifted her hands in question. "My car can use a tune-up. The plumbing in the bakery still sucks. My bed creaks when I turn over. Care to fix those things, too?"

The lift of her lips told him she wasn't angry; she was yanking his chain. He already knew there was no way Katie would pass up a chance to twist his balls.

"Bobby Williams is who you call for car service. Mark MacPherson is the all-around handyman. When it comes to your bed ... I'll be happy to assist."

"I'll keep that in mind if I ever get you past the doorjamb."

She was right; he hadn't set foot inside the bakery since he returned. He tried to mask his frown with motion. After he helped her into the rowboat, he untied it, pushed off the dock, and jumped into the boat himself. Then he handed her the oars. "You wanted to row. Knock yourself out."

How such a little thing like gliding across the lake could give her such a thrill, he didn't understand. She was beautiful, intelligent, and kind. How did the simple joys of life pass her by?

CHAPTER TEN

Who would have thought rowing could be so hard? Katie gripped the handles and pulled the paddles through the water. She'd read about rowing last night, and it seemed simple enough. She had to scoop water and put it behind her. To turn, she simply put the brakes on one side by stalling one oar in the water.

Easy peasy.

"Give me those." Bowie reached for the oars. "You're going to wear yourself out."

Katie gripped tighter. There was no way she'd relinquish her power. "Sit back and enjoy. I'm in charge of these." She raised the handles to prove a point, only to have one of them slip from her hand and slide into the water. "Oh. My. God." She laughed so hard, her stomach ached.

He pointed to the lone paddle in her hand. "Give me that for a minute." The air between them stilled while she contemplated his request. "I'll give it back with the other one once I have them both," he said to reassure her.

She reluctantly handed it to him and watched as he maneuvered the boat close enough to grab the rogue oar floating away from them. True to his word, he handed them back to her.

"Here you go, Duchess. Row until your heart's content."

Katie was certain it was hard for Bowie to surrender power. He seemed like the kind of man who controlled everything he could. She imagined the reason he hadn't been back to Aspen Cove since his fiancée died was that he couldn't control the situation then, and he couldn't control how he felt about it now.

"Sit back and relax. I'm going to give you the ride of your life." She teased him with his own words.

"Don't tease." He stretched out on the wooden bench. His legs were so long, they extended and tucked under her seat.

"I can't believe rowing is on your bucket list. What happened to things like meet a movie star or drive a Maserati?"

Katie made sure the oars were firmly in the ring thingy, then leaned forward and dipped them into the water. It took more strength and energy than she expected to pull them forward, but she wasn't a quitter.

"I've driven a Maserati. It belonged to one of my doctors."

"You've mentioned doctors more than once. Care to elaborate?"

"Not really. I was a sickly kid and spent a lot of time in the hospital." She let go of one oar for a second to touch her chest. "I had a little heart issue, but it's all good now." She was certain most people wouldn't call heart failure a "little issue." She didn't want to focus on the past. She wanted to live her future. She looked down at the angry scar that sliced through his knee and disappeared under the camouflage print of his cut-off shorts. "What about you?"

"I've seen a few doctors, too." He rubbed his knee and pulled the fabric higher to reveal the wound. "I'm still here. You're still here." He looked around them. The lake was dotted with fishing boats. "Stay clear of everyone else. You don't want to piss off a bunch of old fishermen. They won't think anything of 'accidentally' hooking you with their next cast."

"I got this."

Once the boat moved, she had it. They glided across the water. The still glasslike surface broke and rippled with their movement. Several birds swooped down to see if the couple had anything interesting to offer, and when they found nothing but two people and a plastic bag, they moved on. As she neared a boat ahead, she braked and turned right.

Bowie reached for the bag he'd packed. "Hungry?" He raised a brow. "We can free float while we eat the gourmet sandwiches I prepared."

"Gourmet, huh?" She pulled in the oars and tucked them under the bench. "What makes them gourmet?"

Bowie laughed. "I have no idea, but it sounded good."

"Pony up the goods, mister. I've been rowing, and I'm starved."

"You've been rowing for five minutes." He opened the bag and pulled out two bagged sandwiches and two bottles of water. "So, you still want to share both?"

She rose from her seat. The boat rocked from side to side as she made her way to the space beside him. "I like sharing with you." She for sure liked sharing his kisses. "Most people would share a meal before they shared a kiss. We've done it backward."

"I don't know. Who doesn't like a little appetizer first?"

She took the baggie with the bologna sandwich inside. She reached in, pulled out the two halves, and offered him one. "So I'm your amuse-bouche?"

"My what?" He took a bite of his half of the sandwich—a blob of mustard caught on the corner of his lip.

Katie couldn't help herself. She rose up and licked it away and savored the tangy taste it left on her tongue. "An amuse-bouche is something you eat to whet your appetite. Something to amuse your taste buds until you get to the main course."

"I'm hoping to get to the main course with you soon." He looked at her with heat in his eyes.

"So now I'm the appetizer *and* the main course."

She took a bite of her sandwich. How a bologna and mustard sandwich tasted so good, she had no idea. Maybe sharing it with Bowie made it better. Maybe the way he teased her made a simple sandwich decadent. Who was she kidding? There was no maybe. Everything about Bowie spoke to her.

He nuzzled his face into her neck. The scruff of a few unshaven days rubbed her skin to create a nice, warm burn. The wet of his tongue traced from her collarbone to the shell of her ear.

"You're dessert, too."

A slow trickle of desire oozed like warmed honey through her veins. There wasn't a place on her body that didn't want to be dessert for Bowie Bishop.

"We'll see. Maybe your appetite will fade at peanut butter and jelly." She picked up the other baggie and pulled out her half of the sandwich. "The jelly is sweet and satisfying."

Bowie turned to face her. "I'm sure you're sweet, too,

and I guarantee when I'm done with you, you'll be satisfied."

Every word he said made her shiver, but one word made her heart sink to the worn wooden bottom of the boat. He said the word "done." Which made it sound like once he had her, that would be it.

Though Katie wanted to find love, she had to be realistic. Life was fleeting. Uncertain. Unyielding. Wasn't it better to have the thing she wanted once than never at all? No one knew better than her how life could change. She looked at Bowie, who had turned to glance at the water. He also knew a person could be here today and not tomorrow.

"I'd love to be your dessert." It was a bold statement. One she'd embrace because deep inside, she knew a day with Bowie was better than any day without.

He grabbed the oars and situated them into the rings. "My turn to row. I don't want you worn out before I get you into bed."

"I love how you think."

She took her seat across from him and finished her sandwich. With each pull of the oars, his muscles grew until the cotton shirt stretched tight over his arms and chest—parts of his body certain to be exposed later.

When he turned to look toward the shore, the sunlight glinted off the faded white line that bisected his cheek.

"Where did you get that scar?" She lifted her hand to her unblemished cheek.

His eyes narrowed, and his jaw tightened. The tick of a tense muscle twitched. "Car accident."

Her heart skipped a beat. By the sternness of his reply, it had to be associated with his biggest loss. "I'm sorry. It's none of my business."

They sat in silence for a long minute. He turned the boat so they faced the west side of the lake.

"We'd been together for over ten years when she died." His voice was low and far away. "I've never talked about it with anyone, but I got this scar trying to save her and my mother. I saved neither."

The air surrounding them turned heavy with regret. She wasn't certain how to respond. "You don't have to tell me."

He pulled his eyes from the mountainside to look at her. "I feel like you need to know. You need to understand why I can never love you. Not because you're not lovable, but because I'm not capable of love any longer."

When she swallowed, it was as if a boulder stuck in her throat. "I doubt you're incapable. It's that you're resistant. Why wouldn't you be? Love is risky."

He pointed from her to him. "And you're okay with this, knowing it'll never be more?"

Inside, she wanted to cry for herself and for him. Was she okay with never having the option of more with Bowie? Not really, but she had to be. She knew she deserved more, and so did he, but something told her he was worth the gamble. "You and I both know how fragile life is. Let's not worry about tomorrow. Let's live for today."

He rowed harder until they were cutting through the water like a hot knife through butter. "You make being here better."

"Being here isn't so bad. You might find you like it after all. Heck, you might even stay." *A girl could hope*.

She watched the scenery pass as Bowie propelled them forward.

"My mom used to say, 'Never cross the same bridge twice.' I've crossed this bridge before. I'm not staying."

She tilted her head to the side and made a face. "Really? Neverisms? I hate them."

He pulled in the oars. They coasted across the water. "What are you talking about?" He put his elbows on his knees and leaned forward with his hands clasped between his legs. "Neverisms?"

"You know. All the stuff people spout off like it's sage advice. Things like 'Never look a gift horse in the mouth' or 'Never moon a werewolf.' What the heck is a gift horse? And do werewolves exist? Wasted words packaged like wisdom."

"Some of them are good."

"Tell me one that's been beneficial to you."

He sat there. She could see the gears turning in his head, and she knew by the way his lips rose in the corners and the light in his eyes sparkled, he'd thought of one.

"Never say never." He gave her a look that said, *beat that.*

"You just said never." She shook her head, exasperated that he'd contradicted himself. "I'll give you this; that's the wisest one of them all because it leaves your options open. The one about the bridge ... what if what you wanted or needed was on the other side of that bridge? Would you cross it then? If you didn't ... you'd never know."

A breeze picked up. A man in a nearby boat hooted and hollered in celebration of his latest catch. The sun had fallen on the horizon and sat above the peak. The last remnants of snow had melted away. Bright green Aspen leaves colored the mountainside. It was spring, a time for new beginnings.

"You're right. Neverisms are stupid," Bowie said.

"I hate to make a blanket statement on anything, which is why 'never say never' is good. There are a few others worth mentioning, like 'Never pass up a chance to say I love you' or 'Never lose a chance to say a kind word' or 'Never let a man rowing your boat get away without a kiss.'" She launched herself at him, knocking him over.

For the next twenty minutes, they lay on the floor of the boat and made out like teenagers. It wasn't until a brave bird landed and pecked at the empty sandwich bags they came up for air.

The sun barely peeked above the mountain, which meant in no time it would be dark. "We should get back." He turned the boat around and moved toward shore. "Let's go home and get changed and meet back at the bar for a drink tonight."

"Is that all you want? A drink?"

"I never said that was *all* I wanted."

She licked his taste from her lips. "You sure like that word 'never.'"

"I do," he said with confidence. "Here's one more for you to think about. I'm going to do things to you tonight that will make certain you never forget me."

Playfulness looked good on him. It was nice to see him relax and enjoy the moment. So when he flashed his white teeth in an open-mouthed smile, something inside her melted like chocolate on a sun-warmed sidewalk. She thought of a "never" of her own. Never had she wanted a man as much as she wanted Bowie.

CHAPTER ELEVEN

The twenty minutes it took to get to the bakery were glorious. Her arms wrapped around his waist. Her head pressed against his back with him cradled between her open thighs. He hated dropping her off.

Once she walked inside, he took off for home with a promise of later. Her last words to him were, "Don't shave."

A girl like Katie should be with a banker or business-man. What she wanted with someone like him was beyond imagination. He had nothing to offer her. Seeing as she was a grown-up, he decided not to question it.

They'd talked about a lot of things on the boat when they weren't kissing. How she'd worked as a data entry clerk for her dad's insurance company. How her parents didn't give her much space to make choices, and why coming to Aspen Cove had been the scariest and best decision of her life.

He'd shared some things about himself. Never before had he offered information about *that day*. His heart and lungs seized when he looked across the lake to where it all happened, then he looked at Katie, and everything loosened up. She was human Xanax.

Just as he arrived at home, his father walked out the door. The smell of aftershave hit Bowie head-on. "Got another date?" He couldn't fault him for wanting to share his life with someone.

Ben shrugged his shoulders. "I don't know what's wrong with Maisey, but she's good to me." He pulled out his wallet and looked through his bills.

"You got enough money?" It was funny how the tables had turned. Once upon a time, it was Bowie standing in front of his father penniless.

"I do. Enough for dinner and a movie." His dad put his wallet away. His head dropped to look at the ground. "I may not be home tonight. Will that bother you?"

Bowie stood a foot taller than his dad and leaned down to look him in the eye. "I want you to be happy. Does Maisey make you happy?"

Ben's head rose. "I'm happier than I've been in a while. You're home. Your brother's got a good woman. I've got a job I like. Katie is special." He looked at the motorcycle sitting in the driveway. "Was that her I saw on the back of your bike?"

His dad didn't miss a thing. "I took her for a ride to the lake. She wanted to row a boat."

Ben laughed. "'Special' might not be the right word. She's quirky, but she's cute. Don't hurt her, Bowie. I have a feeling she's been through a lot already."

Bowie looked past his dad to B's Bed and Breakfast. "Haven't we all?"

Ben pulled his son in for a hug. He'd been uncharacteristically touchy-feely since Bowie had come home. "I love you, son. It's time for you to be happy, too."

Bowie nodded and walked backward toward the house. "Have a good time. Glove it before you love it."

"Get in the house," his father said with mock sternness.

Bowie headed straight for the shower. When he emerged smelling like soap instead of sweat, he ran into Cannon.

"Coming to the bar tonight?" his brother asked.

"I'll be there. I'm meeting Katie for a drink."

"Is that right? You got the hots for her?"

"She's hot, but it's not like that." It was exactly like that, but he wasn't fessing up. "We're friends. That's all."

Cannon stood in his doorway, buttoning his shirt. "Don't mess with her. I don't want Sage mad at me because you screwed with her best friend."

Bowie threw his hands in the air. "Why does everyone think I'm going to hurt her?"

Cannon shrugged. "Because you might. But don't. I'll kick your ass if you do." He brushed past Bowie. "I'm running late. I'll see you there."

He heard the front door close before he entered his room. While everyone around him had changed, his space had remained the same. Stuck in a time warp. The dresser was covered with memories, from the wheat back pennies Brandy gave him to movie stubs and brochures for wedding venues.

He picked up the advertisement for a place called The Chateau. It sat on the edge of Silver Springs. A cross between a dude ranch and a spa, and it had been Brandy's top choice.

He picked up the trash can and, with one swipe, threw it all away. There was no use holding on to the past. It never made him feel good about the future. There was another "never" for him to consider.

Could he have a future? Would his heart ever soften enough to let someone in? He couldn't see a time when that would happen. His future didn't hold a place for love, but it had a slice of time where he could hold Katie.

HE WATCHED the door for over thirty minutes, but she didn't show.

"Got a date?" Doc asked from the stool next to him. "You're watching that door like you're waiting for someone."

"No, not a date, but Katie's coming by to have a drink with me."

Doc folded his napkin into a grid of nine. He was on his second beer, which meant he'd be playing tic-tac-toe with Cannon to see who paid.

"Back in my day, if a girl said she'd meet you for a drink, that was considered a date. You youngsters are confusing."

"I'm not the dating type." He pulled the beer to his lips and took a drink. The cold carbonation helped tamp down the fire he'd built inside. Just thinking about Katie made him smolder.

"She's a good girl, that Katie. She's—"

Having heard it before, Bowie finished the sentence. "I know, she's special, and if I hurt her, you're going to kick my ass." He tipped back his frosted mug and took another drink.

Doc looked at him, perplexed. "I was going to say she's a blessing to Aspen Cove, but you're right, she is special. I'm too old to kick your ass, but there's a dozen people around her who will if you hurt her." He laughed and finished his beer.

Cannon walked over and started with an O in the center of the grid. Bowie ignored the rest of the game and kept his eyes on the door. A few minutes later, she walked inside. Dressed in tight blue jeans and those damn red boots, every eye in the place was on her.

For a Sunday, the bar was full, but it was tourist season, and the people of Aspen Cove financed their entire year in the months of May through October.

He hadn't noticed before, but the idiots from earlier were playing pool. The stupid blond guy whispered to his friends until they all turned to stare at Katie.

She paid no attention to them. Her eyes were on him, and he'd be damned if that didn't feel good. He was broken and damaged and scarred and ugly, but she looked at him like he was a prince.

"Hey," she said. She climbed onto the seat next to him and smiled. "You beat me here."

He turned to her. She was stunning. Her hair was the lightest blonde, and it looked white under the lights. Her skin, flawless. Her lips plump and kissable. She smelled like strawberries and honey. He wanted to pull her into his arms and taste that sweet mouth of hers, but that would be like claiming her as his own. She wasn't his. He wasn't hers.

"You want the usual?" Cannon asked.

It bit at him that his brother knew what her usual was. Bowie knew very little about this woman, except she was beautiful and kind. She had been sickly as a child. Had overprotective parents and few life experiences. He knew her skin felt like satin, and her mouth tasted like honey. Her desire for him was as strong as his for her. She had curves that fit against him like a laser-cut puzzle piece. Her touch calmed him. That southern twang in her voice was like music to his ears.

Cannon placed a soda on the counter in front of her.

"Soda?" Bowie asked. She looked more like a wine girl; then again, who knew? He didn't really know her.

"I love the bubbly water."

She was a puzzle. "So let's play a game."

She clapped her hands. "I love games." She looked past him to where Cannon stood, losing a game of tic-tac-toe. "You want to play that?"

"Hell no. I want to get to know you," Bowie moved closer and whispered in her ear. "Before I get to know you." He pulled back.

An appealing blush highlighted her cheekbones. He liked knowing he put it there.

"What do you want to know?"

He reached up and brushed a piece of hair away from her eyes—those beautiful, soulful blue eyes. "I want to know everything, so let's play a game I call truth or lie."

"I know this game. You want to go first?"

"Ladies first, Duchess."

Katie sipped her soda water. "I'm turning eighteen next month."

Bowie choked on his beer. "I pray that's a lie because if it isn't, I'm going to jail tomorrow."

She laughed. "I'm twenty-eight, but my birthday is next month. Your turn."

"I've been shot seven times."

She chewed her cheek and stared at him. "I'd say that's the truth. Do I get to kiss your scars?" Her voice was soft and low and seductive.

"I'd love to feel your lips on me."

Doc rose from his stool and gave a wave goodbye. Cannon brought another pitcher of beer to the jerks at the pool table.

"I recorded a record when I was fifteen." She sat there with a straight face.

Bowie wasn't fooled because even though her face was solid and serious, her hands tapped nervously on her knee. That was her tell. She was a terrible liar.

"Lie."

"How did you know?"

He leaned back against the counter. "I'm intuitive." He fed her the same words she'd given him the day they met.

Over the course of the next hour, they learned a lot about each other.

She ran three times a week.

He spent three months in a hospital after his last injury.

She had a younger brother and sister.

He had Cannon.

She loved sweet potatoes.

He loved eggplant.

She'd always wanted a dog.

He wanted a new Harley.

She loved lip gloss.

So did he when he tasted it on her lips.

She loved reading about romance.

He loved *Penthouse*.

She liked bad boys like him.

He liked her.

When the jukebox played, she pulled him to his feet. "Dance with me. I love this song."

He didn't recognize it, but she told him an artist named Indigo sang it. They found an empty piece of floor, and she fell into his arms while the moving voice of the artist sang about unfulfilled wishes and dreams.

Moments later, the blond idiot poked him in the shoulder. "Mind if I cut in?"

Bowie laughed. "You really have a death wish, don't you?"

"I'm just asking you for a minute with a pretty girl." He looked at Bowie's scarred face.

"I don't mind stepping aside as long as you don't mind castration." Bowie looked down on the man. He was stupid but brave. "You come near her again—in fact, if you even look at her, I'll rip your gonads free and feed them to you. Got it?" He pulled Katie into his arms. He loved the way she naturally curled into his side. "Let me give you some advice. Here in Aspen Cove, there are rules. You don't jump on someone else's ride. You don't fish in another man's pond. You don't touch another man's woman. This one is mine."

He nodded toward his brother, who was watching from behind the bar, then led Katie out the door.

What the hell did I just do?

He'd claimed her.

CHAPTER TWELVE

"Would you have really fed him his ... what did you call them ... gonads?" Katie walked close enough to Bowie to be considered a piece of him. Every one of her curves slipped into the notches of his body. He nestled perfectly beside her.

He stopped in the center of the street and looked down at her with a lazy smile. "I would have ripped them out through his throat as a warning to others. You are not the girl to mess with." He leaned down and pressed his mouth to her forehead. Lighting-laced lips sent a jolt through her that made every nerve ending tingle.

Although he was easily eight inches taller than her, they seemed to be perfectly matched.

"For a guy who wants nothing more than a good time, you sure put out the possessive vibe." She tilted her head to look at him. "When you're done with me, I'm never likely to get another date in this town."

The hard line of his jaw twitched. "Tonight, you're mine. I'm a selfish bastard, and I refuse to share." His big palms cradled the back of her neck as he leaned down to kiss her.

The man fried her brain with his touch. "Tomorrow, I'm free game?"

He wrapped his arm around her waist and led her to his truck. "We'll see." When they got to the passenger side, he opened the door and helped her into her seat. "Let's live it a minute at a time." He covered her mouth and stole a kiss.

Her heart galloped at a pace that left her dizzy. She'd been kissed by plenty of men but never had her heart want to leap out of her chest and live inside theirs until now.

She pulled away. "Who knows? By tomorrow I might be done with you."

She doubted every word that came out, but it felt good to say it. He'd been telling her since they met that all they'd be together was a good time. There was no questioning that fact. If Bowie could turn her insides to goo and her brain to stone with a kiss, who knew what he could do to the real estate between her legs? But part of being independent meant she got to decide, too, so she reminded him he wasn't in control of her or how this moment would turn out.

"That's a possibility, not a probability." He closed the door and walked around the truck to his side.

She liked the easy confidence of his walk. Bowie wasn't out to prove a point. She doubted very much he'd fret over her pleasure. He held an air about him that said he knew he could please her. That kind of confidence was sexy as hell.

"Your place or mine?" Katie buckled her seat belt.

"Mine. No one will be home tonight. Dad's at Maisey's, and Cannon basically lives at B's."

She turned her body to face him. "Won't that be hard for you?"

He made that warm, soft sound that wasn't quite a

laugh but something closer to a growl. It sent shivers racing down her spine.

"No, but give me a few minutes, and I'll be hard for you."

She reached over and playfully punched him in the chest. "You know what I mean."

A moment of silence stretched between them as they drove the few blocks to his house. He pulled into the gravel driveway and killed the engine. He unbuckled his seat belt and shifted his body to face her. The uneasy expression in his baby-blue eyes showed the turmoil he must have felt inside.

"I won't lie to you and say it'll be easy, but we've got this place or your place, and I'm not ready for the bakery."

Katie felt a deep need to comfort the man she knew was hurting inside. She slid to his side of the bench seat and crawled into his lap. "I want to help you through this. I want you, Bowie. I want this moment with no expectations of more. Let's forget about the world and get lost in each other. Surely, the universe can grant us a few minutes of pleasure." She rested her hands on his tense shoulders. Her fingers kneaded the taut muscles.

"A few minutes?" His shoulders shook with his laugh. "You don't have much confidence in me, do you?" He swung the door open and slid out of the seat with her wrapped around his waist. She loved the way his hands cradled her bottom and pulled her body close to his. The ease with which he held her made her feel light as a snowflake. "I've learned not to expect much."

With a bump of his hip, he shut the door. Three long strides got them to the front porch, two strides up the steps, skipping several as he went. A quick stop to unlock the door. Several steps down the hallway to a room that smelled like him.

She looked around at the walls covered with classic rock posters. A lava lamp sat on his dresser, with the blob of blue oil drowning at the bottom.

"Welcome to the nineties." He lowered her to the edge of the bed. "Just pretend we're in one of those joints that rent themed rooms." He glanced around the space and shook his head. "I was never one for decorating."

Katie rose from the bed and walked to the poster of No Doubt. "I don't know ... Gwen Stefani knows how to make a room pretty."

Bowie snuck up on her and buried his head in the crook of her neck. The scruff of his unshaven face roughed up her tender skin in the most delicious way.

"You make my room look pretty."

"Flattery will get you ... everywhere." She turned around and pressed her hands against his hard chest. Her fingers traced his muscles from his pecs to the start of his beard. "Glad you didn't shave." Once her hands were wrapped around his neck, she pulled him down for a kiss. She wasn't usually so bold, but this was the new Katie, the one who went after what she wanted, and right now, she wanted Bowie.

He turned them around and walked her back to the edge of the bed. The mattress hit the back of her knees and folded her back on top of the soft blue comforter.

"Everything comes off but these boots. They're sexy as hell."

She pulled her lower lip between her teeth and chewed. She hadn't given this much thought. Sure, she'd fantasized about Bowie and her in bed since the day they met, but to actually be here with him looking at her with eyes filled with liquid lust was a different story. She felt completely unprepared for the emotions and sensations he stirred within her.

The last time she dated a guy, they made it to the fifth date. She thought being honest about her condition was prudent, but when she told Samuel she was a heart transplant recipient over dinner, he folded his napkin and stood. She thought he was going to the bathroom, but fifteen minutes later, he hadn't returned. When she asked for the bill, the waitress said the gentleman had paid and left.

He took two days to text her. "I can't be with someone so broken." That was the first time she realized she viewed herself differently than the rest of the world. Whereas her ten-inch scar spoke of weakness to others, it spoke of strength to her.

She never considered herself broken; she thought of herself as fixed. Broken was when, at twenty, she lay in the hospital without the energy to press the nurse call button; today, she could run for miles at a stretch. The only thing broken was Samuel. Right then, she decided that telling someone about her illness weakened her position in the relationship. Then again, she didn't want to strip her shirt off and shock the hell out of Bowie.

"I'll take everything off but my shirt and boots."

He shook his head back and forth. "No way, Duchess. I've been dying to see those breasts of yours."

"Fine, but I'm scarred." Like ripping off a Band-Aid, she said the words quickly, hoping it would take the sting out.

"We're all scarred."

He reached for the hem of her shirt and pulled it over her head. She watched as he took in every bare inch of her body. His eyes lingered on the black lace that barely contained her breasts. Sitting perfectly between the two lace cups was a long, thin, silver scar that ran from the top of her breastbone to the bottom of her ribs. He took her all in, but not once did he look disgusted, or worse, filled with pity.

"You're perfect."

Those were words she hadn't expected or prepared for. If she didn't fall more in love with him, then nothing would pull her heartstrings. "Glad you're blind."

"Oh, sweetheart, I see what's important." He traced her scar with the tip of his calloused finger. "This doesn't tell me what you aren't. It shows me what you are. You're one badass, sexy woman." His thick fingers unhinged the front clasp of her bra. When it fell open, his eyes, once the color of a spring sky, turned night blue. "I can't believe you've been hiding these from me." He cupped her full breasts with his palms. "I knew it."

Katie lay back while Bowie moved up her body, knees on both sides, straddling her hips. "Knew what?"

"That these were made for my hands."

She reached up to cup the roundness of his chest muscles. "You overflow mine." For the first time, she didn't focus on her scar because he didn't. It was like he didn't see it. "Take your shirt off." She didn't recognize the throaty growl to her voice.

He sat back with his firm butt pressed to her thighs and crossed his arms, gripped the hem of his shirt, and slowly pulled the cotton up his chest and over his head. Katie sucked in a breath at his beauty. Sure, he was scarred like her, but every one of his scars represented a battle with life and death. A battle from which he came out the victor.

Her fingertips skimmed over his battle scars. A long gash across the right side of his chest. An indent to the left of his happy trail. A jagged line that ran the length of his right side.

He placed his hands over hers and moved them down his body. "Knife fight." He left the gash and lowered their hands to his side. "Shrapnel from an IED." He unbuttoned and unzipped his pants, leaving the two sides to fall open. The indent bled into another scar that disappeared beneath the denim. "Bullet wound and surgery." He let her hands go and leaned over her, his lips a breath away from hers. "They don't define me." He adjusted his body. The hot stroke of his wet tongue ran down her scar. "This doesn't define you. You are beautiful."

His lips and tongue continued their path until the denim of her jeans stopped his progress. Her entire body vibrated with need. On her elbows, she lifted and watched him tug her button open with his teeth, then quickly move the zipper down. She drew in a ragged breath and willed her heart to slow its pace. She couldn't think with the whoosh of blood sounding in her ears.

While he tugged the tight jeans over her hips, she heeled off her boots. If he wanted her in them, he could put them back on her. Distracted by her pants, her red boots were forgotten.

What started off as a languid taste of her skin turned into a frenzy of clothes flying in all directions. She pulled at his pants until they bunched around his ankles. He hopped up and out of his jeans.

God, he was magnificent. A body carved in stone. Her eyes took him in from the top of his cropped hair to the rigid length of him curved up toward his stomach. For a woman who was practically virginal for her age, he didn't frighten her. With only two solid experiences under her belt, she could have been struck by nerves. Instead, she was consumed by need.

He blanketed her body with his. The coarse hairs on his

chest tickled the sensitive buds of her nipples. The scruff was back at her neck, moving against her skin in what could only be described as practiced seduction.

"You like this?" He jutted out his chin and rubbed back and forth across her chest.

"Oh, yes." A sexy sigh escaped her lips. She loved it. She wanted to feel that texture on her skin until he left her chafed and burning. "Kiss me."

"Gladly." He moved up her body, the length of him sitting heavy between her thighs. "I love your lips and your taste and that little moan that sounds each time I kiss you."

He covered her mouth with his. His tongue probed at the seam of her lips until she opened to him. The kiss was deep and moving. He wasn't simply kissing her. He explored everything about her, from her taste to her texture. That little moan he spoke of filled the air.

When his hands reached for her breasts, she inhaled sharply. With her shirt-on rule, they rarely saw action; so, when he rolled the puckered skin between his fingers, she arched up to meet his touch.

It didn't take him long to leave her mouth so he could run his hot tongue to the same buds that begged for attention. Searing, he sucked and pulled at them until she was a quivering mess.

She ignored his chuckle as he lowered himself to the cradle of her thighs. "Is this where you wanted to feel my five o'clock shadow?" The heat of his words blew across the sensitive flesh between her legs.

"Yes." She'd experienced the hunger of a man once before and could only say she was a fan. "I want to feel you everywhere."

And she did. Bowie did things to her body she only imagined could happen. He took her from shaking between the subtle strokes of his tongue to the screaming of his name several times. When she lay like a wet noodle in the center of his bed, he hovered over her. The proof of his desire twitched between her legs.

He lifted his head. "What about birth control?" His voice hung low in the air. A bit of gravel and a lot of need made four words sound like continued foreplay.

"We need to use a condom. I'm not on anything." With her condition, barrier methods were less risky.

He rose from her body, leaving goose bumps on every inch of her skin. "Lucky for us, I've got two condoms in my wallet. These suckers have been to several countries." He pulled his wallet from his pants and took out the two foil-wrapped packages.

"How old are they?" Katie knew latex had a shelf life. She had no idea what it was, but she wasn't willing to take chances.

"Less than a year." He lifted the corner of one packet to his mouth and tore the foil open. He held it up to the light. "It looks all right to me."

"Glad you came prepared."

She was glad because she couldn't imagine having to turn back now. She looked at the green condom pinched between his fingers. Why condoms had to come in crazy colors, Katie didn't know. She'd never had a longing desire to be filled with green until that moment. Hell, Bowie's condom could have been any color, and that would have been her favorite.

He rolled it onto his impressive length and climbed between her legs. "You ready?"

She gripped his hips and pulled him to her entrance. "If I said no?" She shifted her hips, pressing him inside of her a fraction of an inch. She watched his eyes narrow as he rode the razor's edge of self-control.

"I'd ask you why. If I couldn't get you ready, then I'd lie beside you and hold you. I'd never force you into anything."

She hiked up her hips more. "I'm ready."

He heaved a sigh of relief. "Oh, thank Christ." With firm control, he pressed inside her.

White-hot lightning raced through her veins the minute he was fully seated inside. She reached around and gripped his firm globes and pulled him deeper. This wasn't about the sex. It was about the connection between them. She already knew the sex would be phenomenal. What she didn't expect was to have her heart sing when they were fused as closely together as possible. If this was all she would get—this one moment in time—she wanted to feel him as deeply as a person could. If she only got this one night, the memory would have to last her forever.

"So good," she whispered into the crook of his neck.

While his body stroked hers, she thought about how he'd told her he wanted to make sure she'd never forget him. There wasn't a chance of that. This moment would go down in history as the best sexual experience of her life.

"You're made for me, Katie. So damn perfect." His pace increased, and so did her passion.

Heat rose from her core to her heart, then slammed back to her core in what only could be described as implosion. She shattered beneath him while he continued to take her places she'd never been. When she whispered his name, he stilled. Time stilled. Everything stilled. In that second, she knew that, despite his warnings and her lies to herself, she would fall in love with Bowie Bishop.

CHAPTER THIRTEEN

Bowie turned and reached for Katie, but the spot where she had been curled up beside him was empty and cold.

"Katie?" he called. "Where are you?" He stilled and listened, hoping to hear movement from somewhere in the house, but it was silent.

He lifted his leg into the air and flexed it. Mornings were the worst. After the time he'd spent on his knees cradled between her thighs, he expected his body to scream at him, but the opposite was true. Rather than feel like his leg was cast in stone, he had the range of motion he'd only dreamed about. Sure, the muscle was sore, but in a good way.

He rolled out of bed, and into yesterday's jeans, tugging them up his legs. After a glorious night of passion and pleasure, he should have felt buoyant, but heaviness weighed him down—she was gone.

He checked the house for her, hoping maybe she was in the shower or on the back deck, but nope, she was nowhere in sight.

He plodded to the kitchen and popped a K-cup in the

coffeemaker. While it filled the room with a comforting smell, Bowie was anything but comforted. He thought about the woman who had called out his name all night long. Each time she said *"Yes"* or *"More"* or *"So good"* or *"Bowie,"* the wall he'd erected to protect his heart had cracked and then crumbled. By the time they fell asleep, his emotions were raw and bared. Everyone around him said Katie was special.

He couldn't pinpoint why that was true, but it was. There was an odd mix of strength and vulnerability to her.

He picked up his coffee and held it to his lips. The clock on the stove read six in the morning. He thought of the bakery. Not in the sad way he'd always remembered it, but in a utilitarian sense. She hadn't left him in bed because she wanted to. She left him because she had to. That made the sting of waking up alone less painful. He only wished she'd woken him to give her a ride.

The front door opened, and in walked Cannon. His hair stuck up in every direction.

"Why are you up so early?" Bowie asked.

"Hans is in town, and we're going fishing." He swept past him and started a cup of coffee. "Do you remember him?"

Bowie laughed. "Exchange student that knocked up the Paisley girl so he could stay in the country? I remember him. He's still around?"

"Yep. He planted a lot of seeds around town. He's almost as bad as Bobby for breeding, except Bobby plants his seeds into the same garden plot, whereas Hans likes a lot of different plots of land."

"What's wrong with these guys? I've got one word —condom."

Cannon's coffee sputtered to a finish before he brought

the steaming cup up to his lips for a drink. After a satisfied sigh, he said, "Speaking of condoms ... was that Katie I saw leaving this morning?"

Bowie would not feed his brother any information that could be used against him. "Don't know what you're talking about." He turned and looked out the kitchen window. A slight breeze moved the pine needles back and forth.

"All right. If that's how you want to play this, it's fine." Cannon walked over to Bowie. Side by side, their shoulders touched while both men looked forward. "Just wanted you to know I approve. She's perfect for you."

Bowie's throat tightened. His body went rigid. "You got it wrong." Although he said the words out loud, each one tasted like the lie it was. Katie was perfect for him, but was he perfect for her? How could she settle for so little when she deserved so much more?

"Maybe, but I saw you last night. I've only seen you that way with one girl."

"Those guys were assholes."

"They are assholes. The same assholes that just extended their trip for two more days. Why do you think I'm staying with Sage?"

Bowie laughed. "Because you get laid? Because she feels good in your arms at night? Because you're in love with her?"

Cannon gave him a you've-got-me-there look. "Guilty of everything."

"Just marry the girl and get it over with. You and I both know time waits for no man." Bowie walked away from his brother and took a seat at the table. "If she's the one, seal the deal."

Cannon walked over and leaned against the wall of

windows that looked out at the lake. "Do you think there's only one for each of us?"

There was a time Bowie knew that to be the truth, but it was before he kissed Katie Middleton. "I think you know when it's right in your heart. If you can't imagine a life without her or her life without you, then I'd say she's the one. If your life would be less without her in it, then she's the one. If seeing her again after just leaving her is the most important thing in your day—"

"I know, she's the one." Cannon kicked off the wall. "The assholes are getting ready to go hiking and said something about picking up a muffin on their way."

Bowie flew from his chair and raced to his room to get fully dressed. In the background, he heard his brother's laughter.

All he thought about as he drove down Main Street was if one of those idiots was anywhere near Katie, he'd be wearing a fist to go with his polo shirt. He parked right in front of the bakery. There were a half-dozen people in line, and he scanned the men but came up empty. They were all locals stopping by on their way to work.

Bowie remembered a time when Aspen Cove bustled with business. Back when the paper mill was open. The air always smelled like fresh-cut wood, no matter what time of year you came to visit. Main Street was always busy, and there wasn't an empty house in sight. When the Guilds abandoned the mill and that Victorian Mansion on Daisy Lane, everything changed. Both buildings were like ghosts of the past.

He sat in his truck and watched Katie. She had a smile for everyone. He couldn't hear what she was saying, but he watched those lush lips move. Lips that had given him so much pleasure the night before. He was stupid to think he'd be able to get her out of his system with one night. Hell, the first time he kissed her, all he thought about was the next kiss he'd get. He contemplated the words he'd told his brother. Could she be the one? Brandy was the one. She'd always been the one, but now, here was this girl who charmed everyone in her presence, including him. Did he dare consider the possibility he'd been given a second chance at love?

Out of the corner of his eye, he saw the three douchebags stumble from their Porsche Cayenne. Before he could exit his truck, they were already in the bakery.

Bowie was torn between leaving the past behind, which meant not stepping back into it, or protecting his chance of a future, which meant steamrolling into the front door.

He stood on the sidewalk, one foot pointed in the direction of the bakery, one foot pointed toward his truck. What he did right here would decide everything.

When the bakery emptied except for the three men and Katie, there was no choice. She belonged to him.

He marched inside the building and came around the back counter to stand beside her. "You should have woken me up, Duchess. I would have driven you here." He looked straight at the blond man and smiled before he turned Katie around and kissed her hard on the lips. "I missed you."

Bowie slung his arm over Katie's shoulder. A sign of possession. "What can I get you boys?" He emphasized the word "boys" because he knew it would irritate the men. "My brother says you're hiking today?"

"Your brother?" the brown-haired man said. "Is he the Neanderthal that runs the bed and breakfast and the bar?"

"That would be the one." Bowie snapped together a box like he'd done it all his life. Then again, he'd spent many an afternoon boxing up muffins just waiting for Brandy. "Muffins? Coffee?"

While he waited for their answer, he looked around the place. The layout was the same, but it didn't feel familiar. He expected it to be heavy with loss and sadness, but it was bright and happy, like the woman who stood next to him, looking at him like he'd lost his mind.

"Three muffins and three coffees."

Katie turned to start the coffee while Bowie boxed up the muffins. "My girl makes the best muffins in town."

The men were quiet. Bowie plopped the muffins inside the box and shoved it across the counter. "If you boys are looking for some action, you won't find it here. I'd suggest you look in Copper Creek. They don't have the caveman mentality you'll find here."

Katie's shoulders shook with her suppressed laugh. "Here you go." She rang up their order and took the money. After the three men left them alone, she turned to Bowie. "What was that all about?"

She rocked forward, then rocked away from him. He couldn't blame her. He'd sent conflicting messages since he'd met her. Telling her all she'd be was a good time wasn't fair. She was that. The best time he'd had in years, but she was more than that. His heart ached for the way he'd reduced her to nothing more than a pleasurable act. Bowie knew then he had a lot to make up for.

"That was me telling them you aren't available. Me telling you I had an amazing time last night. And me also telling you you're more than a good time."

She breezed past him into the kitchen. She dumped eggs and butter and vanilla into the large stand mixer. "This is me telling you I have to make more muffins." She walked up to him and stood on her tiptoes to press a kiss to his lips. "Me telling you that last night was amazing. Thanks for making me feel ..." She paused for a minute. "Whole."

She went about her business like he wasn't there, and for the first time in a long time, Bowie felt uncertain. He'd always been the one to make the rules. He gloved it, he loved it, and he disappeared. With Katie, he couldn't imagine a day without seeing her smile. He wanted to wake up next to her and feel the heat of her body clinging to his. He wanted more, and that scared the hell out of him. More was dangerous.

"Can I take the last muffin?" He looked over his back to the display case that held heart-shaped cookies, mini cakes, and one muffin.

"Knock yourself out." She hefted the large mixing bowl to the prep table and tilted it to its side while she scooped batter into cups. "Grab coffee, too."

He leaned against the doorjamb and watched her. She looked right in the shop. She felt right.

"I never thought you'd set foot in here." She picked up two muffin pans and breezed past him to the oven. The door handle he'd fixed years ago had come loose. He made a mental note to fix it again.

"This wise woman taught me that neverisms are stupid, but I like them. My new mantra is 'Never say never.'"

"That's a good one."

He looked past her to the back door. "How did the apartment upstairs turn out?"

Her eyes opened wide. "You haven't seen it?" She wiped her hands on the apron tied around her waist.

"No. It was only a thought at the time. Brandy had wanted to convert the upstairs to an apartment where we could live. She thought it would be convenient while I ran the bait and tackle store and she ran the bakery, but it never came to pass."

"You're welcome to look around." She stocked the counter with boxes and opened a fresh packet of napkins. "It's a great place, with two bedrooms and a bathroom. There's a small kitchen and a living room. It's perfect. Go on up and see it for yourself."

Bowie shook his head. "I'll wait for the personal tour."

Katie stopped what she was doing and came to stand in front of him. "That would mean you'd have to spend more time with me."

"Duchess, after last night, you'll be lucky to get rid of me."

The way her smile lit up her face made his insides heat. If she didn't have muffins in the oven and he didn't have to open the shop next door, he'd carry her upstairs and start the tour with every surface he could have her on.

"Is that right?" She closed in on him and pressed her hands to his chest. "I once experienced something hard to get rid of, but I'm sure it was a virus."

Bowie laughed. "That's me. I'm a virus you're not likely to shake off too easily."

The timer beeped, and Katie pulled the oven door open. The heat surrounded them both, but Bowie wasn't certain the air whooshing from the oven caused it. "You better leave before I close up shop and beg to be infected again."

"How about dinner tonight at the diner? Just you and me?"

Katie put her hands on her hips. "Bowie Bishop ... are you asking me on a date?"

He smiled at her. "I am. What's your answer, Duchess?"

She flung herself into his arms, hopping up and wrapping her legs around his waist. "One hundred times, yes."

"I'll be at your door at six." He relished the feel of her sliding down his body. She said he made her feel whole. She made him feel alive.

He gave her one last peck on the lips before he walked out. The rest of the day, all he would think about was their next moment together. Deep in his shredded but healing heart, he knew she was the one.

CHAPTER FOURTEEN

Three batches of muffins and ten dozen cookies later, Katie leaned against the counter, exhausted. The only thing that kept her going was the promise of a date with Bowie. A real date. For a man intent on a one-and-done experience, he sure changed his tune. Katie laughed. Maybe Grandma Pearl was right when she advised Katie to tempt men with the china before letting them drink the tea.

Bowie had gotten to know her before she spread out her good china and served her teacakes in the same night. Thinking about her grandma made her think of her mother. Hadn't she made her suffer long enough?

She dialed her mom's number and pressed send. It rang twice before her mother answered.

"Princess ... is everything okay?"

Katie had been called "Princess" long before Kate Middleton came on the scene and landed her prince. She couldn't remember a time where her parents hadn't used the moniker.

"Hello, Mama, how are you?" It was nearing three

o'clock, the slowest time of the day for Katie, so there would be no interruptions. "How's Daddy? Isabella? Nick?" She listed off her siblings in order. Isabella was four years younger than Katie. Nick two years younger than Isabella.

"Everyone is fine, sweetheart. How's the weather?" Over the last two months, her mother had learned not to come out of the gate with *how's your health*, but Katie knew that was always her mother's biggest concern.

"It's wonderful. The skies are healthy. The clouds are rested. It's a beautiful, healthy day."

"I miss you, baby. We got your package. Your sister is just gaga over that lavender lotion you sent."

Katie watched as a family walked into the dry goods store. "It's made locally. A woman in town raises bees, and she uses the honey and wax for amazing things like lotions and candles and soap."

"You're liking Colorado?"

The minute she mailed the box, her location would be known. "I do. I like it so much."

Katie could hear the scrape of a chair on a wooden floor in the background. She could picture her mother sitting at the large stone island in the big country kitchen, looking across the massive back yard of their estate.

"Tell me about your life there." It was the first time her mother acknowledged that she had a life anywhere but Dallas.

"I'll tell you everything as long as you promise not to hop on Daddy's jet and fly here."

Another thing she had told no one was that she came from a wealthy family. Not new money rich, but old family Rockefeller rich. Her great-granddaddy made his money in oil. Her father made his in insurance.

None of that mattered to Katie because when she left Texas, she left it all behind. Being independent didn't mean dipping into the trust fund the minute things became bad. It meant living within her *own* means.

That first day she met Sage and told her she didn't have money for supplies, she wasn't kidding. She'd left with the cash she had in her pocket, which was barely enough to get her to Colorado.

"I promise. Tell me everything."

She moved from behind the counter and took up a chair in front of the window. It was the perfect perch to people watch. She told her everything, from the pink envelope to her muffin of the day.

"You own a bakery?"

"I do, and it's the most wonderful thing to mix up the ingredients and earn money for my masterpiece."

"Your father said you were keeping up with your insurance payments. You know we would have paid them, regardless."

"Don't you understand? I needed this. All my life, I've been Sophia and Tate's daughter—the poor thing with the heart condition. Here in Aspen Cove, I'm just Katie. No one knows about my heart. They don't know my net worth. All they know is, I'm a girl who came to town and learned to make treats. I love being normal."

The bakery was silent except for the hum of the exhaust fan above the oven. "I can see the allure, but you have to tell someone there about your health. What if—"

"I know, Mama. I'll tell someone soon, but for now, I feel great. I'm happy for the first time in years. I've even got a date with an amazing man. I want to pretend I'm normal for a little while longer."

"You've got a date? Who is this boy, and what does he do?"

"At thirty-four, he's a man, not a boy." Katie relived in her mind the things Bowie did to her body last night. No boy would ever have those skills. A shiver of excitement raced through her at the possibility of a repeat tonight. "He used to be a soldier but was injured and returned home."

"What does he do for a living?"

If Katie had been home, her parents would have had a dossier on Bowie. "He runs a bait and tackle shop." She could imagine her mom's eye roll. Sophia Middleton would never approve of Bowie Bishop. He wasn't white-collar and rich. While Katie was privileged, Bowie was a commoner.

"He's a good man. Works hard. Loves his family."

"A bait shop?" Leave it to her mom to hear what she wanted.

"Yes, he taught me how to fish. He went rowing with me. We ate bologna sandwiches. I'm doing things I only dreamed about."

"You could travel first class around the world. Why are you settling for bologna?" She could almost see the curl of her mother's lip. The look she made when she tasted something foul.

Katie let out a frustrated growl. She'd spent a good portion of her life in a hospital. Never once did her parents' money buy her health or happiness. When her heart failed, and machines kept her blood pumping through her veins, their money couldn't buy her a new heart. She waited on the list like everyone else.

"I choose bologna. Bologna may be common, but it tastes good. It feels right." They were no longer talking about food but lifestyles. "You're caviar and Cristal. I'm peanut butter and jelly. I always have been. I'm happy. Be happy for me."

"You know what?" her mom said with more joy and resignation than she'd heard in her lifetime. "You've been through hell and back. If heaven is a small town in Colorado, I'm happy you found it, but don't forget, caviar and Cristal will always be waiting for you."

"I love you." She pressed her lips to the receiver of the phone. "I miss you."

"I miss you, too, Princess. You let me know when I can visit you. Surely, there's an airport nearby."

Katie shook her head. One visit from Sophia Middleton would turn Aspen Cove on its ear. That might be worth the visit alone.

"There's an airport where Daddy's plane can land in Copper Creek. I'll let you know when I'm ready."

"Call me next week?"

"Of course." Katie hadn't missed a phone call with her mom yet. Despite her need to be independent, she also needed the reassurance that when push came to shove, her mom would be there for her. "Talk to you soon."

"Katie?" her mom said before hanging up. "I'm so damn proud of you."

Sophia Middleton never cursed, so when she said "damn," it emphasized the importance of her statement.

Katie looked around the old bakery. Although the building was a gift, she'd built her dozen-muffins-a-day business into a hundred-muffins-a-day empire. She was literally rolling in the dough that made her life here in Aspen Cove possible.

AT SIX O'CLOCK, she ran down the stairs to answer the back door. Taking up the entire doorframe was Bowie dressed in black jeans and a gray T-shirt. In his hands was a mixed bouquet of daffodils and tulips. An odd combination of flowers that somehow worked.

"Are you ready?" He turned to the side and offered his arm.

"I need my purse." She started up the steps, flowers in hand, but he caught her by the thin belt cinching the waist of her dress. She placed the buds on the steps by her feet.

"You don't need anything." He spun her around and pulled her into his chest.

"Not true," she mumbled against the soft cotton of his shirt. "I need a kiss."

He circled her waist with his hands and lifted her like a rag doll into the air until her lips were close to his. "You want a kiss, or need a kiss?"

"What does it matter?"

He kissed her forehead and let her slide down his body. "Oh ... it matters. Want comes from a place of selfishness. Need comes from a place of desperation."

With her chest glued to his stomach, she tilted her head back and looked into his eyes. "Which one gets me a better kiss?"

"Are you sure you were a data entry person and not a negotiator?"

"Kiss me." She tilted her mouth to his. "I'm desperate."

He pressed his lips to hers, and holy hell, if it didn't send a bolt of heat and desire straight to her core.

"Like this?" He left her lips and pressed open mouth kisses down the column of her neck until his lips rested on the pulse point.

Katie stepped back and lifted her hand to her heart. It

pounded out a strong tattoo against her palm. "Help me, Jesus." Normally at one hundred heartbeats per minute, her heart raced beyond that now. "Your kisses are deadly."

"Maybe, but you'll die happy." He gave her a panty-dropping smile. She loved when his smile came from inside and lit up his outside. "Let's go. Dalton is making a special dinner for us, being as it's our first date and all."

Moments later, they were seated in the corner booth. Everything was special, from the cloth napkins to the tiny tea light set on top of an overturned wineglass in the center of the table. Bowie opened a bottle of her favorite sparkling water and poured them each a glass.

"You look beautiful," Bowie said. He lifted his glass in a toast. "To our first date?"

She tapped his glass and sipped. The cool bubbles tickled as they made their way down. The whole idea of a first date with Bowie was both intriguing and ridiculous. The curls that lay on her shoulders shook with her blooming laughter.

"Do you think it's odd we kissed before we shared a meal?" She looked around the mostly empty diner, making sure no one could hear her. "We slept together before we had a date?"

Bowie reached across the table and covered her hands with his. "I owe you an apology, Duchess. I told you you'd never be more than a good time. I was wrong. You're more." He rubbed his thumbs over the tops of her hands. Each time he touched her, every cell in her body danced. "My words were disrespectful. I'm sorry."

Dalton appeared with two plates. They weren't the chicken-fried steak blue-plate special on the menu, but a perfectly cooked filet with grilled asparagus and a fully loaded baked potato.

"Save room for dessert," Dalton said before he turned and left them alone in their quiet little corner.

While they ate, Katie thought about his words. "You don't owe me an apology. I was on board. You can't claim to be a victim if you're involved in the crime."

"Maybe not, but you deserve more. I offered so little."

She picked up a spear of asparagus and licked the salty spices off. Bowie didn't take his eyes off her tongue.

"I knew you would be worth the risk." She bit the flowered end of the stem and hummed. "So good."

Bowie's cheeks blushed. "I loved those words last night. That and when you called my name are in a tie for the sexiest thing I've ever heard. Then there's the 'Yes, yes, yes.' That's up there, too."

Katie could feel heat rise to her cheeks. How many times had she closed her eyes today and relived the moments of pleasure he gave her last night? Could she make it through a meal and not want more? Would her feelings be considered wants or needs?

"I need a kiss." The words came out throaty and sexy.

"Need or want?" He laid his silverware next to his half-eaten meal.

"Need."

The way her body vibrated inside was like the withdrawal of a drug. She was a Bowie junkie after one hit. She took a sip of water, hoping the cold carbonation would cool the heat bubbling inside.

He lifted himself from his side of the booth, moved next to her, and licked her lips. "You taste like a strawberry."

Dalton walked over mid-kiss. "Should I pack this shit up?"

Bowie's lips never left hers, but she saw him give Dalton a thumbs-up.

"Will do," Dalton said on the tail end of his laugh. "I see you got dessert covered."

The moment he left, Katie broke the kiss. "Bowie?"

"Yes, sweetheart?"

"Take me home and disrespect me some more."

CHAPTER FIFTEEN

"Mornin', son." Ben walked into the kitchen and pulled a mug from the cabinet. "Sleep well?" He lifted one eyebrow and smiled.

Bowie hardly slept at all, and it had been that way for weeks. He couldn't get enough of Katie. They spent every moment they could together. They worked next door to each other. They dined together each night and loved on each other every chance they got. When she slept, he watched over her and worried.

This was why he'd promised himself he'd never fall in love again. Love did crazy shit to the brain, not to mention the heart.

"Me? What about you?" He reached past his father for a cup and tried to beat him to the coffeepot, but Ben was too quick. He'd already popped in his K-cup and pressed the start button. "You just getting home?" His father hadn't been spending much there, which left the house for Bowie to use as he pleased.

"It's not like I can bring her here. First off, you and Katie seem to have the nocturnal lease on the place. Second,

I don't think I could do that to your mom. This was her house."

Bowie understood that sentiment. Although he'd become comfortable with the bakery, he couldn't bring himself to go upstairs to the place that was intended to be his and Brandy's starter home. To make love to Katie in the apartment would seem disrespectful to Brandy's memory. He knew he was being ridiculous, considering it had only been a drawing on paper when she died.

Bowie picked up his dad's steaming hot mug of coffee and replaced it with his empty cup. "Do you think you'll ever get over the loss?" He leaned against the harvest-gold counter and waited while the machine spit and sputtered out a cup of perfection.

"Get over it?" His dad shook his head. "Nope. How could you?" He walked to the table and took a seat. Reaching into the fruit bowl, he grabbed a banana and peeled it open. "The best you can hope for is to live with it."

Bowie joined his father at the table. He turned his chair toward the window and watched the rising sun shine off the lake. The water was still and reflected the orange glow of the sun like a mirror, making the water look like fire. Only the ripples of feeding fish disrupted the glasslike surface.

"Is that fair to others?"

Ben took a bite of his banana and chewed. A thoughtful expression of calm crossed his face. "Life isn't fair, son." He pulled the peel down and took another bite. As he chewed the fruit, it appeared he chewed on his thoughts, too. "Was it fair you got shot? Was it fair life took away your mother and your fiancée on the same day? That your father turned into a drunk? You can't worry about fair as far as life goes."

Bowie pulled in a deep breath and exhaled. "I know life isn't fair, but I want to be. Am I being fair to Katie?"

Ben chuckled. "Katie seems pleased with the arrangement."

In the distance, Bowie watched a rowboat cut through the water, leaving a wake behind. That's what he felt like. Katie had cut through the calm he faked. Everything inside him felt unsettled and turbulent in a good way. She made him want more than mere existence. He wanted her.

"When I'm with her, I'm so happy, Dad. She's amazing. We have so much fun together. It's all so easy and so hard at the same time." He leaned back in the chair and kicked up his feet on the empty chair beside him.

"You deserve happiness, Bowie. You're too young to be alone. Hell, I'm too young to be alone."

"Being alone is safe."

His dad shook his head. "That's what I thought, too, but it's not safe. Being alone is simply lonely."

Bowie looked out on the lake and spoke in a whisper. "It's in the quiet moments when I struggle. I watch her sleep, and my gut twists because I'm afraid to lose her, too. Letting her in was dangerous."

Ben sat his cup down and reached out to Bowie. He laid a solid hand on his shoulder and kept it there. "How many purple hearts do you have?"

"Three."

"You didn't get those because you were afraid. You got them because, despite the danger you faced, you dove in headfirst." Ben squeezed Bowie's shoulder before he dropped his arm. "How many bullets did you take?"

He knew where his father was going with his line of questioning. He'd taken seven bullets, but not one hurt as much as the hole shot through his heart when Brandy died. "I don't know if I could handle another hit like that, Dad."

Ben sighed. "I get it. I've lived your pain. I tried to

drown mine in alcohol. You tried to erase yours with adrenaline. How'd that work out for you? My solution got me a pickled liver and a bad reputation. What'd yours get you?"

"A few medals and a lot of scars."

"All I'm saying is, you're not the kind of man who hides. That was me. I hid behind a bottle. You ran into the thick of things and made a difference."

"I'm no hero." Bowie shook his head so hard, his brain ached. "Initially, I ran into the melee, hoping I'd be able to join Brandy. After a while, I ran in because I wanted no one to feel the profound loss I felt at losing someone."

"How many lives did you save?"

He shrugged his shoulders. "It's hard to say." Bowie lost count of the men he'd carried on his back. The flow of blood he'd staunched with as little as a shoelace. The hands he held while a medevac swooped in for rescue. The faces blurred together, and the names sounded the same. Saving his men wasn't an option—it was what he did.

"Son, you're a hero."

"No, I'm just a man." He finished his coffee and looked down at the grounds in the bottom of his cup. He was as significant and insignificant as one of the little brown specs. It took every single one working together to make a decent cup of coffee. One ground made nothing. He thought of that commercial that said, "An army of one." Everything good in his life came in multiples. There was no army if there was only one. That thought was the moment of clarity he'd needed.

"Do you love her?"

"I'm not sure I'm there yet. All I know is, she makes it easier to breathe. It's so confusing. How did you let go of Mom?"

Ben placed both hands flat on the table and leaned

forward. "I'll never let her go. She's a piece of me. I've tucked her safely into a corner of my heart, where she'll live forever."

"My heart is crowded with two women battling for space."

A crease etched into Ben's forehead. "There's no battle, son. Brandy has a place in your memory and your heart, but she's no longer in your life. How lucky are you to find two women worthy of your love? When it comes to life and death, choose life, Bowie. Katie is alive. Be alive with her. There is something magical about her. She's an angel who came here to remind us how to live." Ben stood and left his son to consider his words.

Bowie sat alone at the kitchen table. His dad was right. Bowie had lived in the past for so long, it had eaten into his future. He had denied himself everything, but he wouldn't deny himself Katie and what they could have. There was still time for them.

He'd spent years trying to hold on to a piece of Brandy, but he had to let her go. Tonight after work, he'd visit the cemetery and say goodbye to his first love so he could make room for his second.

It wouldn't be easy. He hadn't been to the gravesite since the day they buried her. He still had nightmares of the crash and how the icy water seeped into the car while he tried to open the doors. His dreams were always silent, except for the gurgle of water exchanging places with oxygen in the car. He broke the window and tore his cheek, trying to get them out. On the frozen shore, he covered them with his bloodied body, hoping to warm the death from their skin.

His mom had been gone since impact, but Brandy somehow hung on to life by the thread of a brain stem. She lingered in the hospital for three days, all but dead without the help of modern medicine. He never understood why Bea waited so long to let her go when the doctors said there was no hope. It was as if she expected resurrection on the third day, and when it didn't come, she pulled the plug.

He shook the macabre memory from his mind. That was the past. He looked at the sun dancing across the lake, at the birds swooping down to feast on a floating bug. The wildflowers were in full bloom. Today was the first day of the rest of his life.

EXCEPT FOR A FEW stolen kisses at the back door, Bowie didn't see much of Katie that day. She'd been busy baking cookies for a church group that was using the old campgrounds for a daytime youth retreat. Heart-shaped cookies covered every surface in the bakery. It was fitting because Katie had such a big heart. She never failed to offer a kind word, a warm smile, or a hug to whoever needed one.

He told her of his plans to stop by the cemetery to say his goodbyes. She looked both relieved and concerned. Before he left, she held him for a long time. In her embrace was where he found hope and courage.

When he arrived at the cemetery, he visited his mother first. On top of her headstone were trinkets his dad or Cannon had left behind. There was an arrowhead, a carved wooden angel, and a roll of cherry Life Savers. Mom used to say they were almost as good as a kiss.

He kneeled before the headstone and plucked at the weeds growing around his mom's favorite yellow flowers. He felt like an awful son for staying away so long. He told her about everything that had happened since she went away. Although there was no answer, he imagined her soft voice telling him it was okay.

Bowie moved several rows to where Bill, Bea, and Brandy were buried. Sprouts of green grass filled in the area around the new headstone. Three cement hearts sat intertwined. An inscription that read, "Gone but not forgotten," was etched in black in the stone. He dropped to his knees and leaned his forehead against the cold granite marker.

"Where do I begin?" He took in several deep breaths to clear his mind. "I think I loved you the day I met you. The day Bill and Bea adopted you. You were six, and you had me tied around your little finger. Who knew I'd be so easy to catch? Then again, I was only eight. We had a comfortable kind of love, the kind you get from knowing someone forever. It was everything until you were gone."

He leaned back and rubbed his thumb over her name. Although it was hard to see her name etched in death for all time and eternity, his insides didn't twist and turn with sorrow and anger or loss. He looked at the stone and remembered her with love and friendship.

"I've met someone. I think I love her, but she deserves all of me, not the shrapnel left of my broken heart. Katie brings light to my life. A smile to my face. Hope to my heart. She makes me feel whole. When you died, so did I. When I met her, I was reborn. I'm here to tell you I will always love you, but I have to let you go."

CHAPTER SIXTEEN

One of the many benefits of owning a shop was flexible scheduling. Seeing as how Ben was happy to close up to go to the diner and be near Maisey, Katie could sneak upstairs and change into something clean that didn't smell like snickerdoodles—not an unpleasant smell by any means, but Bowie loved it when she was bathed in the scent of strawberries and honey.

Showered and dressed, she crossed paths with Sage in the corner store. In her friend's hands were two frozen potpies.

"I swear that man's a saint," Katie said with a giggle. "Does he ever tire of Stouffer's?"

Sage held up the two boxes. "These are Marie Callender's. I'm bringing out the big guns tonight." She pointed to the ad copy. "It says right here, 'A Heritage of Homemade.'"

Katie supposed it was a nice change from the frozen lasagna Sage liked to serve. "That's as close as he'll get to real food, I suppose." She walked down the aisle to where the jars of spaghetti sauce sat on a shelf above the pasta. "I can't say I'm offering anything more spectacular." She grabbed the sauce that had meat in it, along with a package of spaghetti.

"Honey, the Bishop boys aren't complaining about what we're offering." She followed Katie down the aisle to where the green cans of Parmesan cheese were lined up like little Italian soldiers next to the other ingredients perfect for Italian food.

To look around the corner store, it would seem like the people of Aspen Cove had particular tastes. The rows were divided by ethnicity. There was the Italian aisle, the Mexican aisle shared space with the Asian aisle. American food actually had two aisles and had everything guaranteed to give a person high blood pressure or indigestion. Who needed ten varieties of Hamburger Helper? She glanced at Sage and swallowed her question. Obviously, Sage did.

"Do you love him?" Katie asked. The two women hadn't really talked about love. Katie had never been in love, so she couldn't be sure what she felt was the real deal.

"I do. It's funny because the first time I saw him, I wanted to throttle him."

"He was a piece of work."

Katie moved to the freezer section to find the ice cream. It wasn't often she indulged in sweets. Funny for a girl surrounded daily by sugary confections. She looked at the paltry offerings and decided Bowie would be dessert. There was no reason to settle for less. That thought shook her because all her life she'd settled for so little—even with Bowie. He was willing to give her his body, but she was uncertain if he'd give her his heart.

"He's at the cemetery today." Katie's voice sounded far away, like someone else was speaking.

"That will be hard for him."

"He said he needed to say goodbye."

Sage leaned on the Little Debbie snack display and sent the boxes tumbling to the floor like dominos. She scrambled to pick them up, but each time she put one back, another came crashing down.

"Oh, hell," she said. "I suppose I'm nervous and excited for you." She got them all lined up. "If he's saying goodbye, that has to be good. Right?"

Marge peeked around the corner and shook her head at the mess they made of her display. "You girls are trouble."

"Clumsy, maybe. Trouble ... not so much." Katie said as she moved with Sage toward the register. Marge's husband, Phillip, sat reading the newspaper.

Katie laid her items on the counter and turned to Sage. "As for saying goodbye? You'd think it's a good sign, but I'm afraid of what could happen."

Phillip rang up her order. She didn't worry about him hearing the conversation because he was basically deaf. He had hearing aids, but he didn't wear them. He said they were uncomfortable, but Katie knew it was because he couldn't stand the sound of Marge bitching at him all day.

"Have things been good? I didn't want to pry, but you seem to spend more time at his place than your own."

Katie closed her eyes and remembered the heat that washed over her body after last night's lovemaking session. "Things are *so* good. That's the worry. He seems to be moving forward, but going there could set him back."

"How long ago did he leave?"

Katie looked at the ridiculous cat clock hanging on the wall behind Phillip. Its tail moved back and forth with each second. "It's been at least an hour."

Bowie had closed the shop around two and left right away.

"Maybe you should check on him."

"Don't you think that might seem invasive?"

Sage reached in the bucket of water at her feet and pulled out the last bouquet. "Bring these to Bea." She pressed them against Katie's chest, leaving droplets of water darkening her pink T-shirt. "You can say you wanted to thank her for bringing you to Aspen Cove."

"He'll see right through that."

Sage smiled. "Yes, he'll see you care." She waved her hand in front of Phillip's face, getting his attention, and pointed to the flowers and her potpies. "I'll get the flowers. You go get your man."

In truth, Katie wanted to visit Bea's grave. She owed the woman who had given her a second chance. She leaned in and gave her best friend a kiss on the cheek before she turned and walked to the door. "Wish me luck."

"Break a leg," Sage called from behind.

When Katie arrived at the cemetery, it differed greatly from the day they put Bea in the ground. The parking lot was empty except for Bowie's black truck, which sat alone in the corner slot. She scanned the area but saw no one. The only things standing were cement headstones.

Mixed emotions swirled inside her, making her stomach do flips. Was it wrong of her to check on him? All she wanted was the best for Bowie, and at that moment, she knew without a doubt, she was it. She'd fallen in love with the man and was infinitely more capable of taking care of him than a ghost from his past.

A part of her burned with jealousy. Who would have pined for her had she died eight years ago? Her mother. Her father. Her siblings. But there was no man to remember his love for her; no heart filled with treasured memories. She wanted that with Bowie. If she could persuade him to stay in Aspen Cove, she had a chance of reaching that goal. He acted like a man who would stay, but he'd never said the words, and words were important, too.

With the flowers in her hand, she climbed out of her SUV and wound around the path to where she remembered Bea's grave.

As she approached, she saw Bowie on his knees in front of a headstone of three hearts blended together. It was a beautiful tribute to a family filled with love. His fingers traced the black etched lettering of Brandy's name.

She knew her decision to look for Bowie was wrong. This was a private moment between him and his one true love. She had no right to be there. When she stepped backward to retreat, her shoe crunched down on a dried leaf. The sound echoed through the dead silence of the cemetery.

Bowie stood and spun around to face her. His expression went from annoyed to concerned to soft. "Hey, what are you doing here?"

Katie took another step back. "I'm sorry." She looked down at the flowers in her hand. "I thought I'd—" She shook her head. She hated to lie. "I was worried about you. I went by the store to pick up something for dinner and ..." She let out a huge breath that vibrated through her chest. "Are you okay?"

Bowie walked toward her, his hands reaching for her shoulders. He gripped them tightly. She was certain he'd try to shake sense into her, but instead, he pulled her to his chest. "Yes, I'm okay."

She buried her nose into the cotton of his T-shirt and took a deep breath. She associated his smell with everything good in her life. Her arms hung limply beside her, but her body pressed into his for comfort.

"I know this is hard for you. I want you to know that as your friend, I'm here for you."

Bowie seemed to laugh at all the right times, even when it was in the wrong place. They were in the middle of a cemetery, the least likely place to bring a smile to a face or laughter to warm a heart.

He thumbed her chin up and connected eye to eye. "I'd say we're more than friends, Duchess." He leaned down and brushed his lips across hers. He looked over his shoulder to the headstone. "This was about being able to move forward—to give you and me a chance at something more. I could never give you my heart if it belonged to another."

Katie could hardly breathe. He wanted more with her. "I hoped we could be more, but I was willing to settle for less."

He placed his hands on both sides of her head. "You really should set your standards higher. You deserve so much more than me."

She dropped the flowers to the gravelly path and wrapped her arms around him. "And you should see your-self as I do. You are so much more than you give yourself credit for."

They stood on the path and held each other. Katie closed her eyes and said a silent thank you to the universe for bringing this man to her. She said a prayer of thanks to Bea for bringing her to Aspen Cove. Her last silent prayer went to Brandy. She had to have been an amazing woman to have locked down Bowie's heart for so long.

He rubbed his hands down her back. "Shall we get out of here?"

Katie nodded but looked down at the flowers lying at her feet. "I brought these for Bea."

Bowie smiled, and the somber atmosphere of the cemetery lit up. "Then you should give them to her." He bent over and picked up the bouquet. He threaded his fingers through hers and led her to the grave. Her eyes followed the newly bloomed grass to the pristine headstone. Under each name were a birth and death date. Bill had died five years ago; Bea this year. It was when she looked at the date of Brandy's death that her heart stilled. It wasn't a decade past, like she'd been led to believe, but eight years ago on the same day her life began again.

Her lungs seized. Her heart raced, then all but stopped. The world spun around her and turned black.

"Katie." His voice sounded far away, like Bowie was calling to her through thick fog. "Katie, wake up, honey."

She moved along the gravel path in Bowie's arms. "What happened?" She looked up to see relief in his blue eyes.

"There you are." He set her down and propped her against his truck while he opened the door. "You fainted."

"I what?" She pressed her memory for an explanation. It all came rushing back. She had Brandy Bennett's heart.

"You fainted. Hit the ground like a cement block." He picked her up and placed her in his truck. "Banged your head good."

She reached up and touched the tender spot on the back of her head. "Oh, Lord." She had a lump the size of Houston forming. "I can't believe I did that."

"I'm taking you to Doc's. I want him to look you over."

She shook her head, but her brain hurt. "No. I'm fine." Her thoughts were scrambled. "I want to go home."

"Not happening until you get the seal of approval from Doc Parker."

"Seriously?" She leaned against the window. The cool

glass tethered her to consciousness. "I'm fine." Her head spun, but her heart ached. Brandy's heart ached.

She was anything but fine. She'd fallen in love with Bowie. Once he found out she had his fiancée's heart, what would happen? She'd never been more frightened in her life.

Even on the day of her surgery, when they placed the mask over her nose and told her to count, she wasn't as scared as today. Back then, she had a life unlived. Now, she had a future to lose.

CHAPTER SEVENTEEN

Katie watched Bowie race around to help her from the truck. He walked her at a snail's pace to the pharmacy.

Attentive and loving now, but would that end the minute the truth was revealed? Did Katie want to reveal the truth? He'd never asked her about her scar. She'd told him she'd been sickly as a child, and they fixed her.

Did she owe him the facts, or was it good enough that she'd given him the gist of the situation?

Doc Parker came out of the back room with a mug of coffee in his hands. "You cleaned me out of condoms yesterday." He sipped at his coffee. "I don't get a delivery until next week. You ever hear of pacing yourself?"

"I'm not here about condoms." That's when Doc noticed Katie. "She fainted and hit her head hard."

Doc moved fast for an old fart. He rushed around the counter to open the door for Bowie. "Bring her on back."

"I'm fine," she said with little confidence in her voice.

"Stop being difficult," Doc said. He turned on the light to the examination room and patted the paper-covered table. "Climb up, young lady, and let me have a look at your melon."

Bowie helped her onto the table. He didn't leave her side, holding her hand while Doc Parker looked her over.

"You're pale, and your heartbeat is too high." He reached into the drawer and pulled out a stethoscope.

Doc must have seen the fear on her face. The pleading in her eyes. She wasn't sure if she was sending the message that said, "Don't do this here, not with Bowie around," but somehow Doc seemed to understand.

"Son," he said to Bowie. "I need to give her a thorough exam, and although I know you've seen the goods, I'm not into threesomes." He nodded toward the door. "See if the bakery has any muffins left. I'll call you when we're finished."

Bowie looked from Katie to Doc. There was a moment when she wasn't certain he'd leave.

"Do you want me to go?" Bowie squeezed her hand.

"I'll be okay." She swallowed the lump in her throat. "Steal a muffin for me, too. I probably didn't eat enough today, and my blood sugar got low." She hated the lie that flowed so easily from her lips.

Bowie narrowed his eyes for a second. Did he see the lie for what it was—a way to get him out of the office before Doc saw her scar and found out her truth? She thought he'd hold his ground, but instead, he pressed his lips to hers in a comforting kiss.

"You know where I'll be."

Doc waited until he heard the bell above the front door ring. "By the look you gave me, I was sure you didn't want Bowie in here. Was I wrong?"

She shook her head. "No. You will find out something

in a minute that I've kept a secret." Katie pulled the hem of her pink T-shirt over her head.

"Holy heavens." Doc Parker took a step back and grabbed the side table for balance. "He hasn't seen that scar?"

Katie dropped her chin to look at the silver line that ran vertically down her chest. "He's seen it." She shrugged. "He never asked for specifics, and I didn't give him details he didn't require."

Doc Parker pointed to the scar. "That's why you have the bakery."

She nodded. "I didn't know until I went to the cemetery today to check on Bowie." Her eyes filled with tears. Her throat ached. "At Bea's funeral, there was no headstone, and you," she shuddered at the memory, "you said they died a decade ago."

"I rounded up. The exact details didn't matter."

"They did to me. I couldn't figure out why she gave me the bakery. I thought for a second I had her daughter's heart, but the timing didn't match because I was told Brandy had died ten years ago. I should have looked into it more thoroughly. Bea put it plain and simple on the page, 'you have a good heart,' she wrote. She would know. I have her daughter's heart," Katie cried.

Doc pulled a tissue from a nearby box and handed it to her. "She did it and told no one." Doc spread his fingers to massage the strain in his furrowed brows. "She donated her organs."

Katie sat on the examination table, exposed in more than one way. "You didn't know?"

He pushed off the table, put the earpieces in his ears, and pressed the cold cone to her chest. He listened for a while. When he stepped back, his expression was one of awe.

"She never said a word." He wrapped the stethoscope into a circle and put it on the table. "That's a fine heart you have, my dear."

Katie swallowed the lump in her throat. "It's served me well for the last eight years."

Doc Parker went into medical mode. "You have quite a lump on your head." He pulled a light from his pocket and shined it into her eyes. "Your pupils are even, but I won't rule out a concussion." He opened a drawer and lifted a white disk. With a twist, he activated the ice pack and pressed it to the back of her head. "You need to ice that to keep the swelling down."

Katie set the pack next to her while she pulled on her shirt. "Are you going to tell Bowie?" Just the mention of his name made her heart race and her stomach twist into knots.

"No, that's not my truth to tell, but don't you think you should?"

Katie sat for minutes in contemplative silence, or maybe it was shock. "I should."

"But ..." He walked to the sink and washed his hands. He looked over his shoulder at her. "You won't?"

Katie gnawed at her bottom lip. "What if it ruins what we have?"

Doc leaned against the table and crossed his arms over his chest. "What if he finds out somehow? I can't tell you what to do. Your secret is safe with me. It's part of the privacy act, but I think you should be the one to tell him."

Katie nodded and jumped off the table, the movement sending a wave of dizziness rushing at her. She gripped the edge with her free hand to steady herself. "I'll tell him, but I need some time to figure out how."

Doc's bushy white mustache dropped with his frown. "Give it a day or two to sink in." He reached into his pocket and pulled out his phone but set it on the table. "I want you to stay at your place tonight. That way, you'll be close by if you need me. Also, someone has to stay with you to keep an eye on things. Head injuries are tricky. If you showed more severe signs of a concussion, you wouldn't be standing here, you'd be in an ambulance on the way to the hospital." He looked down at the area between her breasts like he had X-ray vision. "Speaking of hospitals … do you have a cardiologist you're seeing? Are you taking your anti-rejection drugs? Where's your family?" He rattled off so many questions, she couldn't keep up.

"I registered with Holland Cardiology in Copper Creek. I haven't seen them yet because I haven't needed to, and I take my meds as directed."

"Good. Good. Derek Holland is a skilled doctor. You couldn't have chosen more wisely."

"He came recommended by my last doctor."

"What about your family?"

"They live in Dallas. They know where I'm at, although they are less than happy with how I got here."

"Do they know?"

Katie wanted to laugh, but she knew it would hurt her already aching head. "How could they know before I did? Donors and recipients are anonymous. I wonder how Bea found me?"

Doc picked up his phone. "I've never known a woman more determined than Bea. She was like a dog with a bone." He smiled. "Wow." He shook his head. "Brandy had never left the state of Colorado until she went to meet you."

Katie lifted her palm to her chest. "I owe her everything."

"Bea used to tell everyone that Brandy might be gone, but she lived in others. We thought she was speaking metaphorically. Like her memories and spirit lived in others. I'll be damned." He punched in some numbers and waited until the person on the other line answered. "She's ready for you, son." He hung up, but his smile burned like a hundred-watt bulb. "What are the chances one man can find the same heart twice?"

The bell above the door rang, and the sound of heavy boots thudded on the linoleum floor in the hallway.

Bowie appeared in the doorway and smiled with relief. "It took you so long, I thought something serious happened."

Doc looked at Katie. "We were chitchattin'. She can tell you all about it."

Katie took a step forward and wobbled. Not that she was dizzy; she was scared. Everything she ever wanted stood in front of her. Bowie had finally said goodbye to Brandy. How would he feel knowing part of Brandy lived inside her?

It was confusing. Almost surreal. For the first time, she questioned her love for Bowie. Was it real? Or was it some supernatural oddity that Brandy's heart recognized Bowie's presence? She'd heard of stranger things.

"I'm ready to go home and go to bed."

"Nuh-uh," Doc said. "No sleeping for two hours." He looked at Bowie. "She needs to be woken up periodically to make sure she's okay. No sexy business either. She needs to rest. Those condoms will hold."

Katie groaned.

Bowie laughed. "I can do that." He stepped forward and wrapped an arm around her waist. "I'll take good care of her." He walked her a step forward.

147

"I want her at her house."

Bowie stopped. He hadn't been inside her house since they met. She wondered if having to be there would pose a problem.

"Not an issue." He looked down at her and whispered. "I let it all go today, Duchess. It's just you and me from now on. I'll never forget her, but Brandy no longer has my heart."

Inside, Katie died a little. They'd never be free of her because although Brandy no longer had Bowie's heart, Katie had hers.

CHAPTER EIGHTEEN

"Put me down." Katie squirmed in his arms.

"Stop it before I drop you and hurt your head again." He'd scooped her up and held her close to his chest. "You weigh nothing."

"Liar." She clutched her arms around his neck and hung on like she'd lose him if he let her go. "I weigh over a hundred pounds."

He cradled her while he raised and lowered her like he was weighing her. "I'd guess one hundred and thirty-two." It was only a guess, but when her jaw dropped, he assumed he was close.

"How did you know?"

Bowie laughed. "In the desert, my rucksack weighed just over eighty pounds without armor or ammo. I used that as a gauge. How close did I get?"

"Off by a pound." She rested her head against his arm and winced.

"Hurts bad, huh?" He adjusted her body so her face leaned into him, not the back of her head.

"It's not pleasant."

Bowie kicked open the door to the bakery. His father stood behind the counter, wearing a ruffled apron. "That's a look I never thought I'd see."

Katie lifted her head and smiled. "He looks good in ruffles."

"What did Doc say?" Ben opened the swinging door that led to the back room.

"He says she needs rest and that you have to run the shop the next few days."

Katie moved until Bowie was forced to put her down rather than drop her.

"He did not. He said he can't rule out a concussion, but that's all he said."

She lifted a broken heart cookie from the cooling rack. He watched her frown before she took a bite.

"Not true. She has to rest and eat well." He looked at his father. "I'll be staying here tonight."

Dad's eyes grew big with his statement. "Oh, okay then."

Bowie winked at his father. "Looks like you and Maisey have options." He'd never seen his father blush, but the red on his cheeks matched the trim on his apron.

"I'm going upstairs," Katie said while she snuck past him.

He reached out and wrapped his arm around her waist, pulling her to his side. "I'll carry you." There was no way Katie was making it up the stairs on her own.

"I can walk."

"Stop being so stubborn. You have a concussion. I'm carrying you." He looked at his dad, who laughed his way back to the front of the bakery.

"I *may* have a concussion. I don't need you to carry me. I don't want you to babysit me."

"Wrong." He bent down and tucked his arm under the crook of her knees and lifted. She crumbled against him. "Doctor's orders." The one thing he knew about Doc Parker was he didn't ask for anything that wasn't needed.

"Fine."

She held on to him while he took the back stairs two at a time. His heart beat rapidly, like a drummer in his chest. He couldn't decide if it was the exertion or the anxiety. As soon as she opened the door, he wasn't sure how he'd feel. This was supposed to be his and Brandy's place.

Though he'd said goodbye at the cemetery. Letting something go wasn't like flicking off a light switch. There were pieces of her that would remain with him forever.

When Katie leaned over to turn the knob, he held his breath. He felt like he was back in Afghanistan, walking through a minefield.

The door swung open, and Katie's sweet scent filled the air. He stopped at the threshold and put her down. The orange glow of the setting sun bled between the cream curtains across the room.

"It's small, but it works." She rocked forward and back-ward several times. He didn't know if she was feeling awkward for him or about him being in her place.

"It's great." He walked past her to the center of the living room. A blue sofa took up most of the space, but the essentials were there, like a coffee table and a television. He moved toward the window, where a small table sat covered with small pieces of paper.

He picked one up.

"Don't read it unless you plan on trying to help." She plucked it from his fingers.

"What are these?"

She pulled a folded piece of paper from a shoebox and

opened it. "This one was granted, or it will be, so I suppose it's okay to share it." She opened the tiny folded square and handed it to him.

My only wish right now is to have an hour alone with my husband so I can show him how much I love him.

Louise Williams

"She wants a babysitter, and you found her one?" Bowie folded the paper and stuck it back into the shoebox.

"I will babysit."

"She's got eight kids."

Katie moved her head from left to right with slow deliberation. "She has seven. Maybe there will be eight if she gets that hour alone with Bobby."

"Don't tell, Doc."

Katie looked exhausted. She pulled out a chair and sat with a heavy thud. "I'm not telling anyone's secrets." She turned from him and looked out the window.

Since her fall, she'd lost her spark. "Beaten down" were words he'd use to describe her. "You look exhausted."

"I'm okay." She rose. "Let me show you the mansion."

Bowie had done all right with the little he'd seen. He didn't need a full tour, but if it was important to Katie, he'd suffer through it.

He looked around the living room. It wasn't anything like he'd imagined. When Bea had talked of the place, Bowie hadn't pictured it to look like a real apartment. In his mind, he saw a loft with open beams and exposed wiring. This place was an actual apartment. It was perfect.

Katie tentatively took his hand. He turned her palm over to see if she'd injured it during the fall. She'd never been shy about touching him, but her delicate touch felt foreign.

"Does your hand hurt?"

She looked down to where his hand covered hers. "No, it's fine."

She threaded her fingers through his and walked him through the tiny kitchen equipped with everything a person needed, from a microwave to a refrigerator covered in magnets. She had a space on the freezer door with cut up magnetic words and letters. Bowie caught his name amidst words like happy, content, and independent. There was one string of words put together, "I love Bowie." Before he could comment, she reached up and mixed the letters and words so nothing made sense, but even if she could erase the evidence, she couldn't erase his memory of it. She loved him. That was all he needed to know.

"There's stuff in the fridge if you get hungry."

"Sweetheart, I'm starved, but not for food." They had been dating for weeks now, but every time he used sexual innuendo, she blushed. With her skin so pale, the pink that rose to her cheeks made her look downright feverish. "Show me the bedroom where I won't be able to make love to you. I want to see the bed that won't squeak under my weight tonight."

Katie moved ahead of him down the hallway. She poked her head into the first room. "Spare." She moved down to the next door. "Bathroom." At the end of the hallway was her room. It smelled like her. "Convent."

A big bed sat against the wall. Bowie swallowed a stone of sorrow that seemed to lodge in his throat. His brother had custom made a headboard for Brandy and him. He wondered what had happened to it. This bed had a simple wooden frame and headboard.

Katie sat on the bed and fell to her side, curling up like a baby.

"Not yet. Doc says no sleeping for a few hours." He

held her hands and pulled her into a sitting position. He understood how a head injury could change a person, but Katie acted like something had stolen her best friend. "You okay? You seem sad or depressed. Is there anything you want to talk about?"

She turned her head, and he could see tears collecting in the corners of her brilliant blue eyes. "No, I'm tired, that's all."

He had to take her word for it because one thing he knew about Katie was, she didn't lie. She was like an open book, and if something was bothering her, he was certain she'd let him know.

"Tell you what. Let's go into the living room and see if we can't grant some wishes." He helped her to her feet and walked her to the table, where she'd been sorting through the tiny pieces of paper.

She opened one note, crumpled it up, and tossed it into a nearby trash can.

"Hey, that's someone's wish you're throwing away."

She pulled it out and handed him a note that said, "I want a twelve-incher." Bowie wadded it up and tossed it back into the can.

"Don't we all." He reached for a new note. "What are the rules?"

"You can't ask for something ridiculous, like a million dollars or a sports car. Most of the wishes are easy to grant, like this one." She picked up a pink sticky note.

I'd like a dozen heart cookies for my birthday.
Lily Dawson

"Or this one." She opened the yellow paper.

Please pray for my daddy. He really needs a job.

"This one is silly but doable."

Please paste a few stars above your door. I told Jackson

that someday he'd kiss me under the stars, but the only place he goes with me is to your bakery in daylight.

Sadie

P.S. This Saturday would be wonderful.

Katie picked up a pair of scissors and cut out a handful of stars.

"You started this?"

"When I was little. I wished for a lot of things. Things I didn't have a right to wish for, like becoming a royal or never getting sick again. I got my wish to skip the chicken pox and my parents bought me the Barbie Dream House, but most wishes went unfulfilled. That's why I started the Wishing Wall."

Bowie sorted the wishes into piles: One was a prayer pile. One was a silly-but-doable pile. The last one was the almost impossible pile. He would have put Louise Williams's request in that pile because no one in their right mind would babysit seven kids. Only Katie and she couldn't blame that decision on a concussion.

"When I told you I was a sickly child ..." She glanced at him and went back to cutting stars. "I didn't elaborate, but—"

"It doesn't matter. I learned long ago not to dwell on the things that can't be changed."

"It could matter. What if it changed everything?"

He leaned back in his chair and watched her fidget with the scissors. "Unless you have a terminal disease, nothing you can say will make a difference. What's the point in talking about the past? It's the past. What we should talk about is the future." He handed her a blank sticky note. "If you could wish for anything right now, what would it be?" He plunked a pen into her hand.

She thought for a few minutes and then wrote something quickly. He swiped it from the table before she could hide it from him. On the note, it said,

Pray for me that Bowie Bishop will love me anyway.

He knew the hit on the head had jumbled her brains. *Anyway?*

He took the pen and scribbled out the word "anyway" and replaced it with "always." He stretched his body across the table and kissed her. "I'll love you always."

CHAPTER NINETEEN

Two days of Bowie hovering over her were enough. Ben watched the bakery while Cannon stepped up to watch the bait and tackle store. Sage wandered over and mothered Katie while Bowie went home for a change of clothes.

"I promised Bowie I wouldn't leave you." Sage stood in front of her with her hands on her hips.

"You'll be across the street getting me a grilled cheese and fruit salad. I'll be fine for the time it'll take you to pick it up." Katie fluffed the pillow leaning on the blue sofa arm. Bowie insisted she lay down. She fought him on his overprotectiveness at each turn, but she always lost. "I'm more likely to die from starvation than a head injury." Katie looked around Sage and flipped through the channels. Daytime television sucked, and since she'd been on a budget, expensive cable wasn't an option, but each time her limited selection came up, she met it with a sense of pride. She'd paid for those stations with her money. Not once had she dipped into her trust fund to pay for anything, including her pricey insurance.

Sage gave her a "You win" look. "Okay, but don't move."

Katie pulled the plush blanket up to her chin. "Not going anywhere."

She glanced at her phone on the table. She'd been waiting for a private minute to call her mom. Although she craved independence, she needed her mom for the tough moments.

"You better not move. I don't want Bowie mad at me." Sage picked up her bag and walked to the door.

When Katie heard her footsteps disappear down the stairs, she called her mom.

"Mama?" She tried to keep her voice calm and swiped the tears running down her cheeks.

"Katie girl, what's wrong?" Panic rose to a high pitch. Mothers had that sixth sense about their children and never failed to pick up the small hints of something wrong.

Even after heroic attempts to temper her emotions, Katie couldn't stop the sobs from breaking free. "I don't know what to do."

"About what, honey?"

"I'm in love with Bowie."

Silence stretched between them.

"His name is Bowie?" Leave it to her mom to focus on the name and not the emotion.

"Focus. I said I was *in love*." Katie sat up and leaned her side into the armrest. "He's so amazing."

"The bait-and-tackle man?" In the background, the sound of a chair scraping against tile echoed through the line. "Let me get coffee."

Katie heard her mother walk around the kitchen of her Highland Park house.

"He's more than a bait-and-tackle man." Katie knew

there was a large dose of sarcasm tingeing her voice, but she needed her mother to pay attention.

"Honey, that's wonderful. All Daddy and I ever wanted for you was to be happy and healthy. So why the tears?"

Katie started from the beginning, where a pink envelope changed her life. When she got to the part about having Brandy's fiancé and her heart, her mother cried with her.

"I want to kill that woman and hug her at the same time." She pulled in a shaky breath. "She gave you life and stress in the same gift."

Katie could picture her mother dabbing at her eyes with a Kleenex so she didn't mar the makeup that took an hour to put on.

"Mama, she gave me everything. A second chance at life. A way to live independently so I wouldn't have to remain childlike in your eyes. She gave me purpose and friends and the greatest man on Earth, but what happens when I tell him? What if he can't stand to look at me because it's just too weird?"

"He told you nothing could change his feelings for you. Give him a chance to prove it."

"I'm so scared."

Her mother let out a long sigh. "You've been scared before and survived. You've faced more in life than anyone I know. This is small stuff compared to dying."

That was the magic of mothers; they put things into perspective. Sophia Middleton taught Katie to look at life from a glass-half-full attitude. Unless that glass had fine champagne in it, then Sophia said it was better to look at it half empty and get in line to have it filled back up.

"What if he leaves me?"

"Then he never truly loved you."

"What if he only loves me because her heart is in me?"

Her mother rarely made unladylike noises. They weren't flattering, but she let out a growl that could scare a badger. "Honey, he said he loved you. He doesn't know that heart, only what's in it. It's your lifeblood that keeps it pumping. The minute that heart took residence in your chest, there was an agreement made. It would provide you with life, but not without your life-giving blood. Her part in your existence is no stronger than yours. You and she are partners for life."

Mom was right. Brandy's heart wouldn't beat without Katie's blood, and Katie's blood could not circulate without her heart. "I love you, Mama."

"You want me to come out there? I'm happy to hop on the plane today." Her voice was hopeful.

Katie teetered on the edge of saying yes, but she said, "No. I have to do this myself. I'll tell him the truth. You're right. If he's as good a man as I think he is, he'll understand. If not, he wasn't meant for me."

"That's my girl. If things don't go the way you expect, I'm here, Princess. I can have Daddy's plane there in a few hours to pick you up."

Katie told her mom she loved her and hung up. She reflected on their talk. Throughout that conversation, her mother never once commented that Katie had a head injury. She smiled to herself because that meant her mother was learning to trust her to take care of her own health.

The tap of Sage's shoes coming up the stairs meant food was here. She'd need to be fortified to face Bowie.

"I'm back." She rushed in the door with her red curls shooting out like flames around her head. "Dalton said to eat it all; he thinks you're too skinny. He added extras."

Katie swung her legs from the couch to the floor.

"Dalton is a cook. He thinks everyone is too skinny. Skinny people don't pay his bills."

Sage plopped onto the center cushion of the couch. She spread out a feast on the coffee table in front of them. "Don't get mad at me. Dalton said the grilled cheese went great with tomato soup. That the fruit was better with real whipped cream and the whipped cream was lonely without his mother's famous cherry pie."

Katie looked at the buffet set before her and knew she'd eat every bite.

"Ran into Bowie and told him I was feeding you. He said he'd be up after he made his supply order." Sage opened her to-go box, which held a burger and fries. "He's worried about you. Said he thinks the hit on the head is more serious because you don't laugh or smile as much." Sage opened her container of ketchup and drowned an unsuspecting french fry in the cup. "I've seen it, too. Do you think we should take you to Copper Creek to get an MRI? Maybe you have a TBI."

Katie laughed at her use of acronyms. Sage used them all the time, and if Katie hadn't spent a lifetime in the hospital, she'd never know what her friend was talking about. "I don't have a traumatic brain injury. I've got a lot on my mind." Katie wondered if she should tell Sage first. It might be a good idea to practice her speech on her best friend.

"You want to talk about it? Is there something wrong between you and Bowie?" Her vivid green eyes showed concern.

"Yes ... I mean, no." Katie dropped her head. "What I mean is, I need to talk, but what I have to say should be said to Bowie first, except I fear that once I say it, he'll take off and never return."

Sage pulled her food box into her lap and turned to face Katie. "That boy loves you. You're the reason he's still here."

Katie slowly lifted her chin. "I may be the reason he leaves. I want to tell you because I need your 'Sage' advice, but you have to promise not to say a word until I talk to Bowie."

Sage chewed on a fry. "When are you going to tell him whatever this is?"

"Soon."

Sage set her food on the table and reached for Katie's hands. "I don't like to keep secrets, but I want to be here for you."

Katie took in three cleansing breaths. She stood up and pulled her sweatshirt to her neck. "I have this scar." Katie had hoped that with Sage's nursing background, she wouldn't have to say any more, that Sage would put the pieces together, but she sat in silence while Katie dropped her shirt into place and took her seat.

"Wow, that's a doozy. Heart? Lungs? Car accident?"

"Heart. A childhood illness that weakened my heart."

Sage smiled. "And look at you now."

"Remember how we sat in the bakery and tried to figure out Bea's connection to me? How she said I had a good heart?"

Katie knew the second Sage figured it out.

"Oh, shit." Her hand came to her mouth. "You couldn't figure it out then?"

Her mouth went Sahara desert dry. "No. I thought it was because I volunteered at the children's hospital. I knew I didn't have Bea's heart. I had no idea Bea had a daughter. Then when I found out about Brandy, everyone kept using a decade as the timeline for her death." She pounded against her chest. "I got this heart eight years ago." Katie pulled her hands to her face. "Eight years isn't a decade. It's eight damn years."

"Oh, shit," Sage repeated. "When did you find out?"

"When you gave me the flowers and told me to go get my man from the cemetery."

"Oh, shit. This is my fault."

Katie shook her head. "No. No, it's not. Whether or not I took the flowers doesn't change the fact that I have Brandy's heart in my chest. I found Bowie at the gravesite that day, and I walked up to him. He had changed. He'd let her go so he could be with me. I was so happy."

"Oh, shit."

"Stop 'oh, shitting' me. I had the flowers, and he walked me to the grave so I could pay tribute to Bea. I saw the date. Brandy died three days after Cannon and Bowie's mother because Bea kept her on life support until they found matches for her donated organs. She told no one she'd donated them. When I saw the date was the same day I got my heart, I fainted."

"Oh ... honey." Sage leaned in and pulled Katie in for a hug. When she leaned back, she smiled. "It's the most romantic thing I've ever heard in my life."

"Or the creepiest." Katie pulled free. "What the heck will he do when he finds out he's dating the girl who has his first love's heart? I even had a silly string of thoughts, wondering if her heart recognized him, and that's why I fell in love with him."

"You love him on your own. Brandy's heart has nothing to do with it." She said the words, but there was a moment when Sage looked unsure. "I don't know what he'll do. I don't know what I'd do."

"You're no help. Right now, I need your 'Sage' advice."

She sat there and looked at her friend, hoping she'd be able to offer wise counsel in a difficult situation.

"You have to tell him. Bowie has a right to know."

The already open door swung wider to accommodate his body. "Tell me what?" Bowie stood in front of Katie, looking for answers.

CHAPTER TWENTY

Katie's face turned white when he walked through the door. He could tell she tried to hide her distress with a smile. A fake smile that didn't reach her eyes. Something was wrong. First instincts told him to run toward her.

"What's wrong?" He rushed to her, cupped her face, and looked into her eyes. The once bright blue had dulled to a stormy gray. "Is it your head?" He dropped to his knees, forcing the coffee table back to accommodate his size. He fluffed the pillow beside her. "Lie down and let me take care of you."

Bowie had all but forgotten about Sage's presence until she stood up from the couch. "That's my cue to leave." She gathered her meal and her bag and was gone before he or Katie said goodbye. He'd never seen Sage move so swiftly. It was like she was escaping.

Katie lifted her hand to his cheek. She always rubbed his scruff. Although she couldn't care less about his scar, the beard she loved had grown to cover it. "I'm fine." Her hand fell to the soft fabric of the couch. Katie turned her body so her back leaned against the armrest and pulled her legs close to her chest, securing everything in place with clasped hands.

"You're not fine. You're as pale as an egg white." He shuffled sideways and sat on the cushion Sage had vacated. "What's hurting you?"

She pulled her upper lip between her teeth. This was always her thinking pose. Not when she was debating between simple stuff like beef or chicken, but the look she got when her mind raced.

"Slow it down, sweetheart, before you chew a hole in that lip of yours." He reached over and thumbed her upper lip loose. "I have a fondness for your kisses. They would be less appealing if you only had one lip."

"So you're saying if I lost something you thought important, you'd love me less?"

He sat back. "Why do I feel like this is a trick question?"

"It's not. I'm gauging your perspective on what's important. You seem to like my lips."

He leaned forward and inhaled her scent, pressing his lips gently against hers. "I like all of you, but these lips ..."

He closed his eyes and remembered the night she was on her knees before him. Her lips wrapped around him. The smell of her strawberry shampoo floated through the air and hugged him.

They hadn't been intimate since her accident. He missed the connection they shared. Despite spending nearly every minute with her since she fainted, he felt a divide between them. It was silly because they were so much more than sex, but somehow when their bodies weren't interconnected, it felt like their hearts were miles apart.

"You need to eat." He picked up her sandwich and offered it to her.

"I can't eat any more." Shaking hands pushed it away.

He looked down at the grilled cheese that was missing a single bite. "You have to eat more than this." Her lack of sustenance could cause her shaking hands, but his mind went back to the conversation he'd walked in on.

"You have to tell him," Sage had said.

She pulled her knees to her chest and rocked back and forth? "We need to talk."

The twist in his stomach caused physical pain from his gut to his heart. Those four words were never good. His mind raced for an explanation.

"Tell me what's wrong. What have I done?"

Her eyes grew wide. "You? Nothing. You're perfect. It's me."

"I'm far from perfect, so what the hell have I done?" The heat of anxiety made Bowie's neck feel like it was on fire. "Nothing good ever starts with 'We have to talk' or ends with 'It's me.'" He knew the flame of his fear rose from his neck to color his face.

Is she breaking up with me?

He'd just let go of his past, took a leap forward, and chose the woman he wanted to spend his future with. He was confused.

"Are we breaking up?"

"I don't want to break up with you. I love you, Bowie, but after what I have to tell you, you may not want my love."

There wasn't one thing he could think of that would change his feelings for Katie. "You can't say anything that will make me love you less."

She laughed. Not the kind of laugh that happened when a person heard something funny, but the crazy cackle of someone a breath away from losing their mind. He closed the gap between them and pulled her into his arms. She folded her body against his and sobbed into his shirt. The last time he'd heard someone cry that hard was when Bea came to the hospital and found out Brandy was brain dead.

Though Bowie needed to know what Katie had to tell him, something gut-deep told him once she did, everything would change.

"I'm scared of losing you, Bowie."

"Not possible."

She pulled away but stayed seated in his lap. "What if you found out something that changes nothing, yet changes everything?"

He tightened his hold on her. His heart raced, and he wondered if she could hear how fast it beat against his ribs.

"I've never been good at puzzles. What are you trying to tell me?"

"Remember the chocolate chip muffins I made, and you said they would be better if I added orange essence?"

"I love the orange essence. It makes them special. Like that added ingredient is the secret to their magnificence."

Though he tried to hold her in his lap, she pushed away and sat beside him. "What I have to tell you may make you think differently about me."

"Jesus, what is it? You have a police record? A handful of kids hidden in the attic? Just tell me."

She pulled in a deep breath and let it out between O-shaped lips. "What if I told you I was a plain chocolate muffin years ago?"

"Not possible. You've got something special. There's nothing ordinary or plain about you. Not now, and probably not then."

"Remember when I said I got sick?" Her hand went to her chest. "It was a rough decade. I spent a ton of time in the hospital. In fact, I was nearing the end of my life, and something happened. I was offered something special, kind of like orange extract, but better."

The constant furrow between his brows made his eyeballs ache. "I've never asked about that scar because I don't care how you got it. Are you telling me you're not healthy? You're sick again?" He couldn't take losing another woman he loved.

"No," she whispered. "I'm not sick."

This had dragged out long enough. "Just tell me whatever it is you think will change my heart. I promise you can't tell me anything that would change my mind about you."

"That's a promise you can't make." She threaded her shaking fingers through her hair and tugged. Her palms covered her face before they fell to her lap. "On April twenty-third, eight years ago, you lost something. I gained something." Her breath quickened. "You lost the love of your life. Because she died, I lived." She placed her hand pledge of allegiance style over her chest. "I have her heart."

Bowie sat stone still. "What?"

"I'm telling you the orange essence in me is Brandy's heart. Sitting in my chest is a piece of the woman you loved and lost."

The world faded to gray before it came back in full color to tilt him sideways. He opened his mouth to speak several times, but nothing came out until his brain could process the enormity of her confession. "You knew and said nothing." He stood abruptly, hitting the coffee table, sending food in all directions. "You knew how broken I was." His throat hurt from the raw emotion. "How could you not say something before now?"

A flood of tears ran down her cheeks. "I didn't know. Not until I brought the flowers to Bea's grave." She fisted her already swollen eyes. "I saw the date, and everything made sense. The bakery, her list, it all came together."

Bowie backed away from her until he ran out of room and hit the wall. "That was days ago. Why didn't you tell me then?"

She fell into the pillow and curled into a ball. "I … I tried, but you said to not dwell on the things that can't be changed. I can't change whose donor heart I received. Nothing's changed."

"Everything's changed." He looked around the apartment and back to the woman he'd fallen in love with. Why wouldn't he still love her? She had the best part of Brandy. "I have to go. I have to think."

Katie rushed from the couch to him and wrapped her arms around his waist. "You said you'd love me always."

Bowie saw the hurt in her eyes. His heart ached for her and for himself. "You prayed I'd love you anyway. You said that because you knew." He pulled free of her hold. "I love you, Katie. I still do, but I need time and space to figure it all out."

She nodded her head and inhaled a shaky breath. "I know … too weird, huh?"

He stared at her, his eyes landing on her chest. "It's creepy." Would he see her as herself, or would he see her as the love he lost? He had to question his feelings for her. Did he fall so hard and fast because he'd already been intimately involved with her heart? Just when he thought he'd moved forward, he was catapulted back to hell. "Give me some time to process."

She stepped back and lowered her head in what could only be described as defeat. "Time would be wise for both of us."

He raced down the staircase and went straight to the

bar, where he knew there would be plenty of alcohol and advice.

Sage was behind the bar when he took a seat on the center stool. "You knew?" He hated that his voice sounded so accusatory, but she was the one pleading with Katie to tell him.

She shook her head. "No, I found out two minutes before you came in."

"Found out what?" Cannon came out of the storage room with a full bottle of Jack Daniels in his hand.

Bowie reached for the bottle and twisted off the cap. "Katie has Brandy's heart."

Sage lined up a few shot glasses.

Cannon stumbled back and leaned on the back bar. "She what?"

The bell above the bar door rang, and in walked Doc. "Saw you running across the street. Thought you might like to chat."

Bowie turned to face Doc Parker. "You knew and didn't say anything to anyone."

He slid onto the stool next to Bowie. With his hands held in the air, he said, "I didn't know, son. She didn't know. No one in town knew. So if you're feeling you've been duped, you best tuck that feeling away because no one lied to you or kept anything from you long term."

Cannon pushed off the counter and came forward, taking the open bottle from Bowie to fill up the shot glasses. "You want one, sweetheart?" he asked Sage.

"No, I think I should go hang out with Katie." She pulled a bottle of wine from the cooler and turned to Doc. "Can she have a glass?"

"A glass won't kill her."

Sage swiped two stemmed glasses from the rack above the bar and walked out, leaving the three men alone.

"So let me get this straight," Cannon started as he pulled beer chasers for the group. "Katie, the girl you love now, has the heart of the girl you loved before. Am I close?"

Bowie tilted his head back and drank what would be the first of many shots. "Spot on." He turned to Doc. "Did you know Bea had donated her organs?"

Doc sipped at his whiskey. "Nope. She never said a word except to say Brandy lived among us. I always thought that was a figure of speech. Like she surrounded us in spirit."

Cannon poured Bowie another shot. "So for real, Katie has a donor heart, and that heart is Brandy's." Cannon laughed. "How damn lucky are you to fall in love with the same heart twice?"

"Lucky?" Bowie tossed back the second shot and shivered as the heat of it ribboned through his body. "It's a freak show."

"Now, now, young man. I won't put up with you calling Katie a freak. I always knew that girl was special. Just didn't know she was extra special."

"Tell me this. Do I love her because I love her, or is it some cosmic thing? Does my heart know that heart?"

Doc rubbed at his bushy brows, making them point straight to the heavens. "Did you love her yesterday when you didn't know she had that heart? Did you ever ask her about the scar?"

"Yes, I loved her, and no, I didn't ask her about the scar; it didn't matter."

"But it matters now?" Doc asked.

"It's different now because I know she has the heart."

Doc finished his shot and turned the glass over on the

table. "She's the same girl as she was yesterday. Let me ask you this. What if you needed a new engine for your truck, and the one that was available came from your dad's truck? Once it's fixed, is it your truck or your dad's truck?"

"It's my truck."

"That there heart is Katie's heart. It stopped being Brandy's when she died. It's just a part, son. We're a sum of all our parts. It's Katie's blood that runs through that heart, not Brandy's. It's Katie's brain that keeps it functioning. Somehow, Brandy's heart found its way into Katie's chest. You would have never known if Bea hadn't given her the bakery. What if Katie hadn't accepted? Is there a little fate happening here? I don't know. All I know is you've got one special woman who loves you enough to tell you. She didn't have to be honest."

"You wouldn't have said anything?"

Doc nodded. "I couldn't. It's doctor/patient privilege. But even if I could, I wouldn't. Katie had to tell you on her own. And she did."

"Two days later." A hint of agitation rose in his voice.

Doc picked up the now-closed bottle of whiskey and tapped Bowie on the head hard enough so he would feel it, but not hard enough to cause damage.

"She had a head injury, you dolt. Let me hit you a little harder and see how clearly you think. That woman has faced death head-on and won. She's happy and healthy and in love. How hard do you think it was for her to risk it all by telling you the truth? That's integrity—another special gift."

Doc looked at Cannon, then nodded to Bowie. "He's paying tonight. I dished out enough wisdom to make it worth a shot and a beer." He picked up his mug and emptied it, the foam sticking to his mustache. "You're a smart man, Bowie; don't be stupid tonight." Doc walked out the door.

"Holy shit." Cannon let out a long whistle. "What the hell are you going to do?"

Bowie held up his shot glass. "I'm getting drunk."

"After that?"

"I'm going to tell Katie I'm sorry."

CHAPTER TWENTY-ONE

Wrapped in Sage's arms, Katie cried herself out of tears. "He looked so broken. I feel so bad." She moved her head to find a dry spot on Sage's floral button-down shirt.

"He'll be back. That boy loves you."

Uncomfortable with a button in her ear, Katie pulled back and looked at her friend. "He loved her, too. If he comes back, how will I know if he's back because of me or her?"

"Oh, honey. You'll know in *your* heart." She pressed a finger forward against the center of Katie's chest.

"That's irony for you. Her heart, my heart, where does one end and the other begin?"

"The heart in you is yours." Sage picked up the bottle and poured Katie more wine. "Doc said you could have a glass. I don't think another half will hurt."

On any other day, Katie would have declined, but she needed to reach the calm that a glass and a half of wine could bring. "I bet you're wondering why I didn't tell anyone."

Sage hopped off the couch and walked toward the

kitchen. "If we're going to get deep, I'll need sugar. Where's your stash?"

Katie followed her and opened the cupboard. She reached to the top shelf for the tub of candy she stashed away for PMS and bad days. If any day qualified as bad, this one did. It was a bad week, and she hadn't opened the tub once. She peeked under the lid, then handed the bucket to Sage.

Sage dug right in. "Ooh, you have peanut butter cups and Skittles. My favorites." She hugged the container to her chest and went back to her seat on the couch. "I'll be good for hours now. Start at birth if you need to go back that far."

For the first time that night, Katie laughed. "You're easy."

"And cheap, but don't tell Cannon."

"He'd love you anyway." Those words came out of Katie's mouth without thought. They were a reminder of the wish for Bowie to love her anyway. She'd hoped and prayed so much, her brain hurt worse than her heart. There was nothing left to do but wait and see if he could come to terms with what she'd shared.

"Bowie loves you. He'll come around. Who knows? We could be sisters someday."

"Wouldn't that be awesome? Do you see Cannon proposing soon?" Talking about Sage's forever made the loss of hers less painful. To focus on joy made it hard to lament her loss. "Do you have a ring in mind? Marquis? Princess cut? Oval?" Katie spent years looking at rings, wedding dresses, wedding venues—things she never thought possible until a donor heart became available.

She'd walked down the aisle a thousand times in her mind. Always dressed in white, she had a long train and a massive diamond that weighed down her hand. She'd trade those dreams for one more ride on the back of Bowie's Harley. One more kiss of his lips. The sound of his voice saying he loved her. Katie shook the thoughts from her head.

"A ring? That man can't afford new jeans. He'd never be able to afford a ring, and I don't care about the ring, but if I could choose, it would be a simple gold band." Sage looked at her empty ring finger. "Big diamonds and nursing don't mesh well. The prong things that hold the diamond tear the gloves."

"You really are cheap and easy." Katie reached into the bucket for a chocolate kiss. It was the closest Katie would get to any kind of kiss, anytime soon. "I saw a beautiful headboard at the dry goods store. It has to be Cannon's work. If it sells, that would buy him plenty of pairs of new jeans and leave enough left over for something special. Maybe a ring?"

"We aren't there yet, but it's a nice thought for the future."

Katie didn't have the luxury of thinking about the future. It would be hard getting through the night. "You know, I considered purchasing it myself. It's so pretty."

"No. Don't buy it." There was nothing playful in Sage's voice. Not a hint of suggestion. It was a demand.

"Why not?" The headboard was beautiful and obviously Cannon's work. Why wouldn't she want it sold?

Sage reached into the candy bucket and pulled out two pieces. She ate them both before she said another word.

"That headboard was Cannon's wedding gift to Brandy and Bowie."

Katie gasped. She was grateful she hadn't bought it. She'd been seconds away from a purchase, but the store only took cash and she was short by several hundred dollars.

"People have to talk in this town," she complained. "I really thought it would look nice in my room. Holy hell, could you imagine if I had bought it?"

"No, but speaking of talking, why didn't you tell anyone?"

"It's not a conversation opener." She took a drink of wine and liked the fruity tang that danced across her tongue. It tasted far sweeter than sorrow. "You don't shake someone's hand and say, 'Hi, I'm Katie, and I have a donor heart.'"

"You're right. Honestly, it's no one's business."

Katie took the candy bucket and rummaged through it until she found a Snickers bar. "The problem is, once people know you're a transplant recipient, they treat you differently."

Sage got a sly smile on her face. "Should you be eating that with your condition?" She exaggerated the worry in her voice.

"Exactly. I was twenty-eight and had to run away from home to get freedom. Do you think I'd let strangers steal it from me? No way. I love being treated like a normal person."

"You are a normal person." Sage shrugged. She dug into the bucket for another fun-sized bag of Skittles. "Then again, 'normal' is a broad term."

"Thanks for making me feel better."

Sage tilted her head and gave a wide smile. "That's what I do; I'm a walking ray of light."

Katie touched a curl shooting from the top of Sage's head. "You're a ball of fire."

"Hair jokes? Just wait until I can Google bad transplant jokes." She popped a green Skittle into her mouth.

The laughter bubbled inside of Katie until she couldn't

hold it back. "I've got one for you. Here goes." She sat ruler straight. "A doctor tells a man needing a heart transplant that the only heart available is that of a sheep. The man agrees, and the doctor performs the transplant of the sheep heart." Katie stopped for dramatic effect. She'd heard it was important when delivering the punch line, and she wanted to make Sage laugh. "A few days after the operation, the man comes in for a checkup, and the doctor asks him, 'How are you feeling?' The man answers, 'Not BAAAAD!'"

Sage tugged the candy back into her lap. "That was awful. Just for that, you get no sweets." She pressed the top onto the plastic container. "Who told you that *baaaad* joke?"

"My transplant doctor," Katie said between bouts of laughter.

"We need better material. You needed a different doctor."

"There's the one about the doctor telling the patient she had her choice of two hearts. A twenty-year-old athlete or an eighty-year-old lawyer."

Sage leaned in like Katie held a secret. "Which one did she take?"

Katie rolled her eyes. "The eighty-year-old lawyer, of course. She wanted the heart that hadn't been used."

Sage tried to suppress her laughter, but a giggle burst forth. "That's so much better. Same doctor tell you that?"

"No. That came from one of my nurses."

"Naturally. Nurses have it all, brains, beauty, and humor."

"I'd love to hear the jokes your sister tells."

"My sister has no sense of humor, especially lately."

"What's going on with her?"

Sage sank into the sofa. "She's entering the last lap of

her residency. There's lots of stress. She expected the hospital to pick up her contract, but maybe it wasn't a good idea to sleep with the boss."

"Does she love him?"

"She thinks she does."

Katie caught sight of her phone's screen glowing. She picked it up and saw the message from Bowie.

Can I come over?

She read it twice. "He wants to come over."

"See, I told you he would figure it out."

The calm the wine provided disappeared. "You did, but I'm not sure how I feel about it."

Sage gave her a confused puppy look. "I don't understand. Don't you want to be with Bowie?"

Katie brought the screen to her nose and inhaled as if she could smell him. It was crazy. She knew she should type "yes, yes, yes," but she couldn't because a question loomed in her mind. When Bowie looked at her from this point forward, would he see her, or would he see Brandy in her?

"I do, but I need to make sure he wants to be with me. The real me." She pointed to her chest. "This little ticker has muddled it all up."

"What are you going to tell him?"

She skimmed her fingers over the screen. "I'll tell him the truth. I need time, too. He's not the only one processing new information." She typed a return message.

Bowie, I love you, but I need time to process all that's gone on. Give me a day or two.

His reply took several minutes.

I'm so sorry. I'll give you anything you need.

"You want me to stay?" Sage asked.

Every possible answer floated through Katie's head. Yes,

no, maybe, but Katie knew no matter how wise her friend could be, given her name was Sage, she needed to search *her* heart for the answers.

"No. I need time to think." Katie rose without giving Sage a chance to change her mind. At the door, she hugged her tight. "Thank you for being here for me. I've never had a friend as wonderful as you."

Sage held on to her for a long minute. "You and I have a bond. Bea chose us. She had a hundred reasons to bring us here."

"Two hundred if you combine them." She gripped Sage's shoulders and turned her body to face the door. "Go find your man. Tell him I promise not to buy the bed if he promises to whittle more ornaments."

"I'll give him the message."

The minute Katie locked the door, her stomach took a turn. It coiled and twisted and tightened. Had she made the right choice? It would have been easier to say yes and fall into Bowie's arms, but easy wasn't always best.

The acid of the wine rose to her throat. She barely made it to the bathroom before she lost everything.

IT HAD BEEN two days since the truth came out—two lonely, awful days where Bowie was so close and yet so far. She heard him next door in the bait and tackle shop, moving things around. She caught him peeking in the window several times a day. Each time she got a glimpse of him, it made her heartsick. She'd never get over loving him and hoped she wouldn't have to because he was everything and everywhere. He was the air she breathed. Above the cinnamon and sugar of the snickerdoodles, he was there in the scent of amber, pine, and sunshine.

Sitting under the Wishing Wall, Katie filled out a pink sticky note for herself. She'd been up most of the last two nights, missing Bowie. Her decision for space was wise, but knowing didn't make it feel better. She printed her wish on the tiny paper and tacked it to the board.

The bell rang above the door. She lifted her head, expecting to see Ben, but it was Bowie in front of her, and he looked worse than she felt.

CHAPTER TWENTY-TWO

"I know you want space, but I had to see you and make sure you were okay."

"I'm okay." She walked past him and behind the counter. "Let me get you coffee and a muffin."

She hadn't kicked him out. That was a plus. The thin line of his lips softened into a smile. "Coffee and a muffin sound great." He leaned against the counter and watched her move gracefully like a leaf in the wind.

She popped a K-cup into the machine and plated up a muffin. "As life would have it, it's chocolate-chip-orange muffin day."

He inhaled the essence of orange. He'd never be able to smell that scent again and not think of Katie. "Unbelievable." He lifted his brow when she handed him the plate.

"Coincidence or fate?" she lifted her shoulders.

"Irony," he replied. Bowie cleared his throat. "You might not know this, but I like orange essence in my muffins."

"I heard that."

"You also might know I love special girls."

Katie leaned across the counter. "What makes these girls special?"

Bowie nodded to the coffee machine, and Katie handed him his cup. He looked to the table under the Wishing Wall. "Will you join me?"

He took a seat at the table, where a pile of wishes sat waiting to be granted. The only wish that hung from the corkboard was hers. He knew because he'd watched her pen it and post it.

"You didn't answer the question." She grabbed a bottle of water from the refrigerator and followed him—another good sign.

"Because the answer isn't short or easy." He pulled the top of the muffin from the base and took a bite. "So good."

He looked at her like she was the muffin. He'd missed her. That first night when he'd asked if he could come over and she said no, he was sure she was punishing him for acting impulsively, but now he knew better. Time to think was important for both of them.

"It's the orange."

"I used to think so, too, but I was wrong. It's more about the surprise. Even without the orange, it would be an excellent muffin. I'd still love it."

He looked at her with as much love as he could convey without touching her. "You would?"

"Yes." He played with the notes on the table and picked one up.

I wish we had a park.

He put it back face up, so the wish was seen. "We used to have a park."

"You want to talk about parks?"

He leaned in and cupped her cheeks. "No, I want to talk about wishes. You want to know mine?"

She handed him a sticky note and a pen. "There's a system here. Follow the rules."

"Never a fan of rules, but for you ..." He jotted down his wish and thumbtacked it to the wall. While there, he removed hers and opened it.

"Hey, that's mine."

"I know, and if I can't grant it, no one can." He opened it and smiled. "Really?"

"What?"

He flattened the note and read it. *I need Bowie to love me.*

"Duchess, I do. I love *you*." He scooted his chair closer and pointed to her chest. "Can I listen?"

His request was odd, but she understood the need. She'd want to hear it, too. It once beat in another chest for him. "Sure." She tilted her head back, giving him room to place his ear to her breastbone.

He pressed his ear to her chest and listened. "Nope. It's not the same." He leaned back and smiled. "This heart is yours and yours alone."

"You believe those words?"

Bowie dropped to his knees, leaned forward, and lowered his head. "After the other night, I know it's hard to believe me. I spent the entire night thinking about a life without you. The you I knew before two days ago, which is the same woman you are today. I'm so sorry, Katie. It was a shock."

"For both of us, but I have to know each time you look at me, you won't see a piece of her."

He lifted his head, so they were face to face. "When I look at you, all I see is love. I see how much I love you and how much you love me."

"We need to talk."

He hated those words. "I don't want to talk. I want to kiss you and make love to you. Are you sure you want to talk?"

"We have to talk. You need to know things about me before you decide if you want to be with me." She wrung her hands together. "I owed you an explanation for my scar. My selfish act of withholding did not give you enough data to decide about a relationship with me."

"I don't need data to know I love you. All I need to know is that you love me in return." He sat up in the chair and leaned back, prepared to sit for hours if that was what she needed.

With outstretched arms, she took hold of his hands. "There are so many factors that can affect our relationship. I got so caught up in the excitement of it all, I forgot to see the reality."

"Are you sick?"

Her grip grew tighter, as if she feared he'd run away, but he wasn't running.

"No. I'm healthy. I've been healthy since the day I got her heart."

Bowie looked at the green cotton T-shirt covering Katie's scar. He forced himself to imagine it was Brandy's heart in there, but he couldn't. Doc was right. Having a part of something didn't make it that thing. "The only reality I see is that we are two people in love."

Bowie flipped his hands, so they cupped hers.

"Okay, but you need facts, and I will give them to you."

"All right, tell me these facts." She tried to pull her hands away, but he held on tight. She would never get away from him again.

"First, I've had this heart for eight years. It's been good. I take my meds every day so my body doesn't reject the gift. I've outlived the average person living with a donor heart."

His heart rate sped up. The blood pounded out a drum-like rhythm in his ears. "You said you weren't sick, now you're telling me you'll die soon?" He'd read as much as he could find on the internet over the last two days. Most of it was beyond his comprehension, but he found many cases where donors lived normal, healthy lives for decades. He'd already decided Katie would grow old. He wanted to see her wrinkle and turn gray with him.

"I don't plan on dying anytime soon. I feel great." She looked around the bakery. "Have you ever thought of your legacy?"

Bowie followed her field of vision. This was Bea's legacy. The bakery would have been Brandy's. "No, in all honesty, I never thought I'd make it out of the desert alive. The universe or fate or God had other plans for me."

"Thankfully. Ben tells me you have three Purple Hearts and a box of other medals and commendations. He says you're a hero. That is part of your legacy." She slipped her hands from his and picked up her water for a drink. "My point in asking is because legacies are stories and heirlooms and assets you pass down to the next generation. Do you want kids?"

Early on, Bowie had thought about a family. He'd wanted children, but when Brandy died, that dream died with her. "It's not something I've thought about in a long time."

"You need to think about it because I can't have kids." She shook her head. "That's not true. I can physically become pregnant, but I shouldn't."

"If you shouldn't, why not go on the pill? We've been using condoms, and although I've never had a failure, they aren't unheard of. In fact, a buddy of mine just had what he calls a 'desert baby.' Blames the condom failure on heat and sand."

"Makes sense." Once the water bottle was back on the table, she leaned forward with her elbows on her knees. "Guys think they are so smart to keep condoms in their wallet, but did you know the constant heat from their body breaks down the latex?"

"Really?"

Bowie considered the condoms they'd used the first night. They'd been in his wallet for a year, survived the squelching heat of a tour in Afghanistan. Thankfully, Katie's cycle had come and gone. She had a short one, but she had one.

"I just told you we could never have kids, and now we're talking about latex and Afghanistan. Don't you want children, Bowie?"

Did he? One thing he knew with absolute certainty was he wanted her; children or no children.

"We'll get a dog. I hear they're less trouble and won't cost us as much over the long term."

Katie rolled her beautiful blue eyes at him. "A dog isn't a son or daughter. It won't carry your name."

"Bullshit. We'll name it Bishop."

"I'm being serious. I come with limitations. I won't ever climb Everest. I won't give you a daughter or a son. I have a compromised immune system. Things can change fast for me."

Bowie pulled her into his lap so she straddled him. "I've never wanted to climb Everest or any other mountain." He dipped his head for a quick kiss. "We'll adopt if having kids is important to you." Another kiss. "I'll take care of you."

"What if things go terribly wrong one day?"

"I've lived through terribly wrong. I survived. We'll do everything we can to keep you healthy. I can live without high-risk activities, but I can't live without you. I love you. Let me show you how much." He pressed his lips to hers, but this time he didn't pull back. The bell above the door rang, but he didn't break the kiss. It was long and lingering. A kiss he wanted to last forever.

"You kids want to take that upstairs?" Ben said as he rounded the counter.

"Yes, we do." Bowie lifted her from the chair.

"Wait." Katie reached for his wish. She plucked it from the board and read it. "I wish for a second chance with Katie. She's my future." She wrapped her arms around his neck. "I can grant that one. I can attest that life is better the second time around."

Bowie adjusted her in his arms and took off for the back stairs. "Call Cannon and tell him he's got the bait shop today," he called over his shoulder to his father. "I'm spending the day with my girl."

When they got upstairs, Bowie took her straight to bed. "I want to make love to you."

She pulled him on top of her. "I want you, too." Her hands went to the button of his jeans. "Too many clothes." The husky, soft vibration of her voice ramped up his desire tenfold.

"Easy to take care of."

He toed off his boots and sent his clothes flying in all directions. Once he was naked, he went to work on her. First, the shoes came off, then her pants and underwear. Bowie worshipped her long legs inch by beautiful inch until he reached the velvet skin of her inner thighs. Oh, how he wanted to stop and spend the afternoon right there, but he had all day, so he moved north trailing his tongue to the edge of her shirt.

"This has to go." With care, he lifted the soft cotton over her head.

It was the first time he'd seen her scar after knowing the truth. As he took in the silver line that ran the length of her chest, she watched him. He knew she was looking for any sign that would tell her he saw something other than her. In the back of his head, he knew it was Brandy's heart that beat beneath her breastbone, but all he saw was Katie.

With a twist, the front snap of her bra unhooked, and the perfect globes of her breasts fell into his hands. Worry clouded her eyes. He needed to reassure her that she was the only one in bed with him.

"I see you, Duchess. Only you." He lowered his mouth to hers, kissed her, and loved the sigh she released against his lips. It shredded him that they'd been apart for days. Wasted precious minutes where loving her could have replaced her worry. "I never want to be apart again. Not even for a day."

Katie stroked his back, tasting his mouth as her hips lifted, searching for his body. He held himself up to keep from crushing her with his weight. He wanted this moment to last forever. A reaffirmation of their love to last a lifetime, but when he released her mouth and looked into her eyes, he saw the fiery heat that erupted between them.

She put her palm against his chest. "Bowie," she said, breathless. His name on her lips filled him with hope and such pleasure. His growing length pressed between her legs.

"We need to protect you, love." He slid down her body, over the flat expanse of her stomach and down her legs. He reluctantly pulled away. Inside her nightstand was a box of condoms he hoped to deplete tonight.

Once he was wrapped and ready, he made his way back up her beautiful body. At her center, he parted her legs and buried his face. Her intake of breath, the sweet sound she made, and the taste of her told him he was home. There was no place for him but with Katie, and all he wanted was to bring her pleasure. She moved beneath his mouth. When her breath went from slow to rapid, he left her little knot of pleasure pulsing and made his way up her body.

Positioned between her legs, he gazed down on perfection. She was scarred. He was scarred. They were made for each other. Although he didn't want Brandy to be a part of this moment, he couldn't help saying a silent thank you for her sacrifice and the gift of Katie.

His mouth captured hers in a soul-searing kiss. He entered her in one deep, slow stroke that caused her to gasp. Her hips rose to meet his with every thrust, and her sighs turned to moans as he moved within her.

It would be so easy to let the passion take over and find his release, but he was determined that her needs would come before his. He pushed and pulled, causing both to breathe harder and faster. The heat of her drove him out of his mind, but he held on steadily while her body sought satisfaction. He wanted more than anything to please her. To replace the pain of the last two days with pleasure. She stilled. Her breath caught as she waited for those shudders of fulfillment to begin. When her sweet voice called out his name, he pressed deep inside her and let the moment of immense pleasure wash over him.

Her breathing slowed, and her body relaxed. Short puffs of air became sighs. Her kisses pressed soft and sweet against his lips.

"I love you," she said.

He fell to her side, lying face to face with his future. He liked the way it looked.

"I love you, too."

They made love so perfectly, so closely, they felt like two bodies with one heart. He hoped his love for her would be etched into her soul because he knew, without a doubt, she had burned her love into every cell of his.

CHAPTER TWENTY-THREE

Doctors' appointments were not new to Katie, but this one was interesting. Bowie had asked her to accompany him to Doc Parker's so he could understand her condition and what his part would be in keeping her healthy.

It had been two days since he carried her into her apartment. She'd never felt so loved or been loved so completely.

"I can see why you didn't tell him." Doc turned to her and lifted his bushy brows.

"Right? Weeks ago I was safe to row a boat, but today he doesn't like me crossing the street by myself." Katie laid a hand on Bowie's back. She knew he was coming from a place of concern and love. "This kind of obsessive behavior made me run away from Dallas."

Bowie's head snapped in her direction. "You run away, I will hunt the ends of the Earth to find you."

"The only running I'm doing is *to* you, but you have to calm down. Tell him, Doc. I'm healthy. I can do almost anything a non-transplant person can do."

Doc let out a long exhale that warbled with the shake of his head. "To be young and in love." He dragged the chair from the corner toward the examination table and flopped into it. "Let her live, Bowie. She can do anything she wants."

"Okay, but she wants to babysit the Williamses' eight kids tonight."

"Seven," Doc and Katie said in unison.

"That's got to be unhealthy."

"Crazy, yes, but unhealthy, no. The Williams children aren't sick. The worse that can happen is they tire Katie out." Doc looked over at her. "Looks like you're doing a fine job of that yourself, son."

Katie felt the heat rise to her cheeks. Now that she and Bowie had made up, they didn't pass up a chance to make love. Doc ordered condoms in bulk and gave them a discount.

"See? I'm good, now stop worrying."

Bowie threaded his fingers through hers. "You can't fault me for wanting to hang on to a good thing. If I'm protective, it's because I love you."

"I love you, too."

"Have you made an appointment with Dr. Holland?" Doc put the stethoscope in his ears. The feet of the chair scraped against the linoleum floor as he stood. He pressed the cold instrument to her chest and listened. "That's a sweet sound." He looked at Bowie. "You want to hear how healthy she is?"

He'd laid on her chest dozens of times, listening to the drum of life beat out a steady rhythm.

"Yes. I do." He turned toward Katie. "If it's okay with you."

She no longer worried about what he would think. He'd proven in short order he loved everything about her, from the way she stole the blankets at night to how she called out his name in passion.

"It's fine. You can listen."

Doc cleaned the earpieces off with an alcohol wipe and placed them in Bowie's ears. She knew the second he heard her heart beating. His smile grew broad and bright. "It so fast," he whispered in awe.

"One hundred heartbeats a minute, just for you."

Doc took his stethoscope away. "I was never one for sickly sweet, but you two are a second away from relationship diabetes. You better grab another box of condoms and go back to bed. You'll eventually get that out of your system, too."

Katie jumped off the exam table. "No time. We've got seven little angels to watch over." She rubbed her hands together like a devious mastermind. "I can't wait to get my hands on baby Bea." Katie had long ago come to terms with the fact that she'd never be a mother, but that didn't stop her from wanting to be one or taking advantage of mothering other people's children.

Doc patted Bowie on the back. "Any more questions, son?"

"I think I'm set."

They walked to the door, and Katie stepped aside to give room to Bowie so he could open the door. She watched the two men exchange glances.

"You gonna open that door, Duchess? I'd hate to take away your independence."

Bowie's grin bloomed until Katie wound up and punched him in the arm.

"Bowie Bishop, I'm not trading my independence for your bad manners."

Doc howled with laughter. "You'll learn, son. Might take you fifty years, but you'll learn."

Bowie pulled the door open. "I need a manual just to learn how this independence thing works."

Katie fisted his shirt and pulled him behind her. "I'll write you one."

They hopped on Bowie's Harley and drove to the Williamses' house. Once parked, they stood outside the two-story Victorian on Daisy Lane. Flower beds bloomed with hydrangeas in pink, green, and blue. A white picket fence surrounded a yard littered with Little Tyke toys. A pang of regret sliced through Katie that she tried to push away. She'd never have this life, but one look at Bowie and her regret turned to gratefulness. She might never hold their child in her arms, but she'd hold him, and that was enough.

"You ready for this?" She buzzed with excitement. Louise said the kids would be bathed and fed, and all they needed to do was entertain them until bedtime.

"I've been to war multiple times. I can't imagine this is worse or different."

She wanted to tell him he was being silly, but his description was spot on. With seven kids to watch, there was no doubt there would be battles won and lost over the next three hours.

Bobbie and Louise met them at the door. Louise looked beautiful tonight dressed in yellow. Little Bea slept in the cradle of her arms.

By the way Bobbie looked at his wife, Katie knew if they didn't stay someplace public, Williams baby number eight would be on the way soon.

"We'll be at Bishop's Brewhouse if you need us." Louise kissed her daughter on the forehead before she passed her off to Katie, who snuggled Bea to her chest and breathed in the scent of baby powder and fabric softener.

It took all of two minutes for the calm of the moment to turn into chaos. Jill ran toward Bowie and threw herself into his arms. Big crocodile tears ran down her cheeks.

"David tore off my Barbie's head." She lifted a decapitated doll to his face.

Bowie's lost expression told her this was worse than war.

David claimed innocence, but the look of guilt shone from him like a beacon. Katie had seen that look of guilt on the faces of many children she'd visited in the children's hospital. When they were stuck in bed, mischief was all they had left.

She shifted baby Bea to one arm and held out her hand. "Give it to me." Her voice was stern despite the laughter that bubbled inside her. "Right now, young man, or G.I. Joe will meet a similar fate." She spied the man-doll gripped in his hand but didn't see the Barbie head.

"She made her doll kiss Joe. He's a soldier."

Lucky for Katie, soldiering was something Bowie could relate to. He gave Jill a hug and put her on her feet. "Go with Katie." He turned to David. "You and I'll talk about women and war."

As Katie herded the kids into the living room to watch a movie Louise had chosen for them, she heard Bowie tell David there were battles a man should wage and some that were better left lost. When David said something about kisses being gross, Bowie laughed and told him he'd change his mind soon enough.

Bowie returned some time later with the doll's head dangling between his fingers. He found the torso discarded on the coffee table. Once he reunited the two pieces, he tucked the doll into the arms of Jill, who had curled into a chair and fallen asleep. He squeezed into the spot next to Katie and wrapped his arm around her.

It took time to get them settled down. For a while, it seemed they all needed something different at the same time. Snacks and bathroom runs and Band-Aids applied to nonexistent wounds took up the first hour of the night. Getting six kids and a baby into the living room was like herding cats. She and Bowie had done it and were no worse for the wear. She looked at the seven children who either slept or zoned in on the cartoon and smiled. They'd survived, so far.

"You know," Katie said to Bowie. She glanced at David, who was lying on the floor, sandwiched between Melissa and Thomas. "You were wonderful with him."

"He's a good kid, and now he's ahead of the pack when it comes to women. I let him know the golden rule."

"There's a golden rule?" Her voice rose with each word. "What's that?"

Bowie seemed to consider whether he should tell her. "I told him the facts. When he's right, he's wrong. When he's wrong, he's wrong. He'll be much happier if he's always wrong. I also told him the right kiss from the right woman would make everything right. Then he and I and G.I. Joe blew up stuff in his room."

Every day, Katie fell in love with Bowie a little more. Her secondhand heart was full. She'd hit the lottery with him and worried he wasn't as lucky with her. It pained her that this man would give up the possibility of a family for her.

"Are you sure you're okay with not having one of these yourself?" She hugged Bea closer to her breast and bent over to rub her cheek along the baby's soft hair.

He looked around the room at the seven kids.

"Watching this brood is the best birth control ever. It's a wonder their parents had time to make so many." Bowie turned and nuzzled his chin into her neck. "If we ever feel like we're missing out, I'm sure Louise will have a new one we can borrow."

"You're probably right, but I don't want you to make a sacrifice you'll regret."

"No regrets. All I want is you."

As the children dropped off to sleep one by one, Bowie carried them to bed. The only one left was Bea, who Katie wanted to cradle for a moment more until her bladder said enough was enough.

"Hold her for a second while I go to the bathroom?"

Bowie stared at the baby as if she'd asked him to hold a live grenade, but he held out his hands and took the tiny little girl. Bowie's arms dwarfed little Bea. She was barely bigger than his palms lined side by side. He looked perfect holding her. Katie stood in the hallway and watched him look down at the baby with wonder and awe. She knew right then her only concern would be never giving Bowie a child.

Bobby and Louise returned, holding hands. They were the kind of couple that emitted the light of love. Katie saw it in the way they looked at their children—the way they looked at each other. She saw the same look in Bowie's eyes when he looked at her.

"Bring that car over whenever you need an oil change," Bobby told Katie before he closed the door.

At the bike, Bowie placed the helmet on her head and said, "You got an oil change for babysitting? I helped. What do I get?"

"I'll show you when we get home." She hung on to

Bowie as he raced back to her apartment, where she expressed her gratitude for over an hour.

They lay sated and wrapped in each other's arms. "We made it through that gauntlet. What's next?"

Katie turned to him. "You thought that was a gauntlet? Wait until you meet my parents. I've invited them here for my birthday."

CHAPTER TWENTY-FOUR

How did this happen?

Bowie sat in the corner booth at Maisey's, waiting for Cannon and his father. Never for one moment in the last eight years did he think he'd be this happy. Although he missed Brandy in many ways, there was more to what he'd found with Katie. She had life experiences that forced her to value the small stuff.

She woke up every morning ready to conquer the world. Her outlook was positive and infectious.

"You want some coffee?" Maisey walked over with the pot swinging in her hands.

"*Need* some coffee is more like it." Bowie overturned the clean cup on the table and slid it toward the edge.

"Late night?"

Bowie laughed. "Early morning." Knowing they wouldn't be sleeping together the next few nights, he and Katie had stayed up making love. It was silly to change their routine because of her parents. They were consenting adults, but he loved her enough to make the sacrifice.

Katie emphasized the point that her very Southern

parents wouldn't be happy about the sleeping arrangements.

"Oh, to be young again." She poured coffee to the brim and slid into the booth across from him. "I wanted to ask you something."

"Anything." Bowie took his first sip and waited for Maisey to continue. He'd never known her to be shy about much, but he saw the vulnerability in her expression. The way she got smaller with each second she waited. "What's up, Maisey?"

"I'm in love with your father, and I want to make sure you're okay with that," she blurted.

"You're in love with my father? That's amazing. You know the Bishop men aren't easy to love."

"Maybe not, but you're worth the effort. Your dad's a good man. More so since he's not drinking. I know it's been a tough time for all of you, but I wanted his boys' blessings before I told him."

"You told me you loved him before you told him?"

She wiggled in her seat. "I wanted to make sure it was okay to love him."

Bowie reached his hand over and touched Maisey's arm. Although she was seated, she looked ready to bolt with her legs facing the middle of the restaurant and her hand still gripping the coffeepot.

"You love who you love. I want my dad to be happy, and he seems happy now that he's with you. I'm sure he would love to know how you feel."

She relaxed against the booth. "Things going well for you and Katie?"

"Well" didn't begin to explain what happened between him and Katie. "She's special."

"Are the rumors true?"

He knew the town would be abuzz about the whole heart thing. It was something people would ask about until the novelty of it wore off. He hoped something more exciting would come up and grab people's attention. For the last several weeks, he'd been busy at the shop, and Katie had been swamped at the bakery. They were a true love story, better suited for television.

"It's all true, but then you know that because you're in love with my father."

She lifted her chin. "I believe it's important to fact-check."

"I agree. Facts are important. Here are a few for you. Katie has a donor heart, but it doesn't matter to me who it belonged to; it's in Katie's chest, so it's hers. She changed my life with her love. I've been given a second chance at happiness. I'd be stupid to pass that up."

"Sounds like you're in love, too." She rocked forward and stood.

"That's a fact."

As Maisey walked away, the door opened, and Ben and Cannon walked inside. Since Bowie took up most of the seat, his father and brother sat across from him.

"Are you nervous, son?" Ben turned over a mug and nodded toward Maisey, who was on her way back with a full pot of coffee.

It didn't pass Bowie's attention when his dad reached out and wrapped his arm possessively around Maisey's waist. He watched his father's expression go soft the minute she looked down at him, and he wondered if he got that same goofy look on his face when Katie was nearby.

"Not really. I'm not sleeping with her parents."

Cannon laughed. "From what I hear, you're not

sleeping with her either." He pushed his empty mug toward Maisey.

"From the way we look, no one is getting sleep." Ben waggled his eyebrows and gave Maisey a pat on the bottom.

She ignored the gesture. "Breakfast special for all of you?"

The three men nodded before she walked away.

Bowie picked up his knife and playfully pointed it at his brother. "If the bed and breakfast had an empty room, they'd be staying there."

"You could have put them at the house, and Dad could have babysat."

Ben shook his head. "The only thing I'm babysitting is that three-legged dog of Sage's. He's about all I can handle."

"Wait until you get some grandkids."

It wasn't public knowledge he and Katie would never have children, so Bowie tried not to react. He would have loved to have a family with her, but it wasn't in the cards. He turned to his father. "Speaking of babysitting, are you good with holding my present for Katie until tomorrow?"

He hoped she liked the puppy he adopted for her. She'd mentioned more than once that she wanted a chocolate Labrador someday. She was never allowed a dog when she was little. He wanted to help her cross off that item from her bucket list. He'd found the furball at the humane society in Gold Gulch. Since he'd rescued the animal, it made little Bishop special. According to Katie, everything and everyone deserved a second chance.

"I'm good. He's locked in the bathroom right now. The little shit got out this morning and ran into the lake. It might be July second, but the water is still cold."

Bowie found it hard to believe he was sitting across from

his brother and his father and all three were planning new futures.

"What about you?" He turned to Cannon. "You got kids on the radar?"

By the look on Cannon's face, a person would have thought he'd been asked to douse himself in gas and light himself on fire. "Oh no, I think I'll wait on that. I like the idea of practicing until we get our routine perfect." He fidgeted with his napkin, which was odd because Cannon was not the nervous type. "I did want to ask you something, though."

There were a lot of people asking Bowie questions this morning. "It's okay if you love her," he said.

"I'm not asking your permission to love her. That's a done deal." He tore at his napkin until it lay in shreds in front of him. "I put that headboard at the dry goods store on consignment, but I should have asked you if you minded if I sold it." Cannon lowered his head.

"Dude, that headboard was a masterpiece. It should be in a museum. I think it's great that you have it for sale."

"You do?"

Bowie nodded. He'd seen it the week before when Katie dragged him in to buy more soap and honey from Abby. She wanted his opinion on a scent, but he didn't care whether she smelled like strawberries or mango as long as she was with him and naked.

"What are you going to buy with the money if you sell it?"

"Money?" Dalton said as he approached the table. "I'll take your money." He put a plate of bacon, eggs, and pancakes in front of each of the three men. Behind him, he reached for a chair and pulled it up to the table. "Who's got money?"

"Not a damn one of us," Ben said. "One thing I've learned over the years is, you never need more than enough. We've got enough."

"Once my disability rating comes in, I should start getting a check from here on out," Bowie said.

"You're getting a disability check?" Dalton asked. "What part of you is disabled, outside of your brain?" He looked at Cannon and Ben. "You two, as well. You're a bunch of wusses for letting women get under your skin."

Cannon coughed on his bacon. "Says the man who went to jail for a woman he didn't know."

Dalton gave them a what-can-I-say shrug. "I'll protect a woman any day of the week, but fall in love ..."

"You will, and when it happens, it's like a Mack Truck colliding with your heart and brain at once."

Dalton looked around the diner. It was filled with locals, but not one single girl was in sight. "You took all the single women in town worth dating." He eyed Ben. "Not that I'd date my mom. That would be all kinds of wrong."

"Things in Aspen Cove are changing. You never know who might show up next," Cannon replied.

Ben swallowed his pancake and took a drink of coffee. "I don't think Bea owned any other property. Doc owns the empty shops on Main Street, so I wouldn't be expecting another pink envelope to steer a woman your way."

Dalton gripped the table. "That's my point. The pickings are slim, and those who are around stay clear of me. Who wants to date a felon?"

Bowie couldn't hide his amusement. It was true Dalton had killed a man, but there were extenuating circumstances. "Any woman who can't see the poetry in what you did doesn't deserve you. You did time for a woman you didn't know. You protected and most likely saved her life. If I were a woman, I'd be asking what you'd do to protect what was yours."

"I'd give everything to protect what was mine," Dalton said.

Bowie patted his friend on the back. "A good woman will know that."

"Speaking of women." Dalton looked between Cannon and Bowie. "Where are yours?"

"Copper Creek," Cannon answered.

"Another Target run?" Dalton reached over and swiped Bowie's last piece of bacon.

Bowie was too slow and couldn't nab it back before Dalton devoured it. "Nope, a parent pickup run. Katie's parents flew in this morning, and she and Sage went to pick them up."

"She hiding you?" Dalton asked.

"No. Since she's been hiding from them for months, she knew they would fuss over her and probably do a fair amount of complaining. She didn't want me to see that side of her parents. Worried that my first impression wouldn't be positive. In fact, she worried herself sick. Sage went along because I asked her to go. I wasn't invited to the homecoming, but I wanted Katie to have moral support."

"That girl domesticated you with efficiency." Dalton lifted his eyes in a challenge to say otherwise.

"Screw you. Your time is coming." Bowie pushed his empty plate to the center of the table.

"Not likely anytime soon." Dalton looked around the diner again. "I better get back to the kitchen." He rose and left the table.

"The plan is still to meet at the bar at five, right?" Cannon stole his father's napkin and wiped his mouth.

"That's the last I heard," Ben said.

Cannon laughed. "Dude, you're meeting the parents. That's huge."

He was right. It was huge. Meeting the parents was almost like buying a ring–something he'd considered over the last two weeks. Instead, he bought a puppy.

CHAPTER TWENTY-FIVE

"Let me get this straight, your parents have a private plane?"

Katie paced inside the tiny terminal of Copper Creek Municipal Airport. It wasn't a terminal as much as a small building close to the tarmac.

"It's a company jet." She pressed her nose to the glass and squinted her eyes. Off in the distance were the lights of an incoming plane.

"What company do they own?"

Katie walked back and forth in front of the glass. "Integrity Insurance."

Sage stepped in front of Katie and stopped her from wearing a path in the carpet. "'The insurance you can trust'?" She sang the jingle that played no less than twenty times a day on the television. "*That* Integrity Insurance?"

"Yes," she said sheepishly.

"Is there anything else you've been keeping to yourself?"

Katie hated she hadn't been completely transparent with anyone. She hadn't lied; she simply didn't divulge more than she had to. Even Bowie didn't know everything. Though he did know her father was an insurance executive, she hadn't painted the full picture.

"I wanted you all to like me for me. I didn't want you to feel sorry for me because of my health issues. I also didn't want my parents' money to be a factor in how people felt about me. To most people, selling insurance is almost as bad as selling used cars. A slimy profession."

"So when you said you were a data entry worker, was that true?" Sage leaned against the glass with her back to the tarmac.

"Yes, I refused any position I didn't earn. I grew up privileged, but I've always wanted to be independent." She looked over Sage's head at the plane touching down hundreds of yards away. "Imagine having to be dependent on someone for everything. That was me, and I promised myself if I got healthy, I'd stand on my own two feet."

"So that's why you drive a piece-of-junk car?"

Katie had bought the SUV used and loved it because she'd done it herself. "That piece of junk is my first large purchase."

"Surely, your parents bought you a car. They're as rich as God himself." Sage fidgeted with her top.

Katie noticed how self-conscious Sage was getting in the minutes since she told her who her parents were. It was the same with everyone. That's why she never said anything.

"Yes, I got a Range Rover for my sixteenth birthday. I was really sick then and couldn't drive it much because my mother was worried I'd pass out behind the wheel. It looked pretty in the garage, though."

"You had a Rover, and you traded it for a used Jeep?" Sage ran her hands through her curls, leaving one coiled toward the ceiling.

Katie smoothed out her friend's hair. "I didn't trade it. It's still in the garage. I think the housekeeper drives it."

"Housekeeper?" Sage shook her head. "You have a housekeeper?"

Katie laughed. "*I* don't. Have you seen my apartment?"

Sage let out an unladylike growl. "I meant ... you grew up with servants?"

The plane pulled up to the building, then a crew walked out to prep for her parents' arrival.

"We had help. You know, like a gardener, a cook, and a housekeeper."

Sage's smile bloomed brightly. "I had you pegged from the beginning as a beauty queen." She fist-pumped the air. "I was spot-on."

Katie smoothed out the wrinkle in the skirt of her dress. "I only won twice. Never got the trifecta."

"So you're rich?"

Katie's sigh sounded like resignation. "Technically, I'm rich. I have a trust fund I don't use." She pointed to herself. "Remember? Independent."

Sage shrugged. "We all need someone. I mean, you took the bakery from Bea. That's not an act of independence."

Katie knew Sage wasn't slamming her for the choice; just trying to figure it out. "I did take the bakery as a way to escape that." She pointed to the couple emerging from the plane like movie stars. Her mother was dressed in Prada, while her dad's suit screamed tailor-made. "Making it work —although not entirely on my own—was as independent as I've ever been."

Sage looked at her. Without warning, she pulled Katie in for a hug. "I'm so proud of you."

"Thank you."

She held her hand to her chest, her heart pounding out

a million beats per second. She knew her parents would hate everything about her new life. She only hoped she could convince them it was right for her.

"I still think it's a shame you have a bunch of money sitting there doing nothing."

Katie smiled. "It's not doing nothing; it's gaining interest. Besides, I have a few ideas on where it could be used."

The door flew open, and Katie's parents walked in. Her mother rushed in for the first hug, while her father stood back and took everything in.

"Oh, honey, it's been too long." Sophia Middleton stepped back and looked Katie up and down. "Have you gained weight?" She walked around her daughter like Katie was on display. "You know being overweight is hard on your heart."

Sage gave her a what-the-hell look.

"Welcome to Colorado." Katie reached out and yanked Sage next to her. "This is my best friend, Sage."

"Nice to meet you, dear," her mom said.

Dad simply nodded in her direction. "Where's the car? We have luggage."

"Luggage? I thought you were only staying for a few days?"

"That's right, but I like to be prepared for anything."

"My place is really small, but it's a forty-minute drive to Aspen Cove, so you'll have time to prepare."

Tate Middleton wielded his wealth like Thor did his hammer. He raised a few bills and asked for help. It was amazing how loud money could speak to some people, but Katie had faced death. Once that happened, she knew money meant nothing.

It was funny to put her parents in the back seat of her

Jeep. She couldn't remember a time where either of her parents were passengers in anything but a limousine.

"I don't understand why you couldn't take the Range Rover," her father said.

"It wouldn't matter; you'd still be sitting in the back." Katie looked to the side at Sage, who tried to hide her smirk. It was obvious she enjoyed this exchange.

Katie's mother leaned forward. "Tell me, Sage, what do you do?"

Sage turned in her seat to face Sophia. "I'm a nurse, and I work in the small clinic in town a few days a week. I also run the only bed and breakfast in town. It was also a gift from Bea Bennett."

Sophia sat up. "Are you a donor recipient as well?"

Sage shook her head. "No. I cared for Bea in her last days."

"Oh, that's lovely." Sophia waited for a minute. "I'm conflicted when it comes to Bea. I'm grateful her daughter was an organ donor. That gift saved Katie's life. However, her other gift took Katie away from us."

Katie knew this trip would be difficult. Her parents were used to getting what they wanted, and what they wanted right now was Katie living back in Dallas in the north wing of the house.

"Bea's gifts saved my life in all ways. I own a bakery, and I have a boyfriend I love. I have friends." She risked a backward glance at her parents, who sat emotionless in the back seat. "I still have you. I love you both, but when you gave birth to me, did you ever truly expect me to live with you forever?"

This time, it was her father who answered. His voice was board meeting serious. "When we had you, all we wanted was a happy, healthy baby. We got that for a while.

Things changed, and so the plan changed. The secret to success is to adapt."

"Exactly. I live in Colorado now; you'll have to adapt." It was so easy to use his words against him. "Besides, you got your original wish. I am happy and healthy. I can't wait for you to meet Bowie."

"That is an odd name. I wonder how he got it."

Sage giggled. "In all honesty, the Bishop boys were named with the first initial of their parents' names, Carly and Ben, but I think Ben had a fascination with armament. He did name his firstborn Bowie, like the knife, and his second Cannon."

"Names always fascinate me. Do you remember that boy you had a crush on in junior high school? His name was Teddy Bear."

Katie remembered him with fondness. "He was a chubby kid no one was nice to but me."

"You always had a soft heart," her father said. "Katie's motto is 'give me your poor, wounded, and downtrodden, and I'll give them my heart.'"

"She has a big heart. There's nothing wrong with showing love and compassion," Sage said in Katie's defense.

"When she was eight, she hid a homeless woman in our pool house."

Out of the corner of her eye, she saw Sage's mouth drop open. "You had a pool?"

Katie smiled. "And a pool boy."

They all but ignored her parents for a few minutes. "Hot?"

"No. Old, but his son was cute. He gave me my first kiss at fifteen."

"He did not. You kissed Manny's son?" Her mother's voice reached the decibel level just below hearing loss.

A giggle welled up in Katie. "Have you seen him? He's gorgeous. Even then, he had the bones of a beautiful man in the making. He was a good kisser."

"Should I be aware of any other help I'll need to fire when I get home?" Tate held his voice in a monotone, but when Katie peeked at him in the rearview mirror, she caught the lift of his lip. He always found her mother's prudish edge funny.

"Don't you know? I kissed them all, even Delia, the housekeeper. Looks like you're going to have to do the dishes yourself from now on."

"Stop teasing," her mother said. "You know I don't do dishes."

Katie glanced at Sage. "Welcome to the Middletons'." All this banter made the drive go quickly. Katie pulled onto Main Street and parked in front of B's Bakery. "This is home."

Her mom pressed her nose to the glass. "You live in a bakery?"

"No, I live above the bakery. Come on." She looked at her father. "You'll have to carry the luggage yourself, Dad. I'm afraid we're servant-free here in Aspen Cove."

Sage hopped out of the car and opened the door for Sophia, who stepped out and looked around like she'd been dropped into the pits of hell.

"This is it? You left Dallas for this?"

Katie was out of the car and on the sidewalk. Her stomach turned, but after this morning, there was nothing left inside it.

"Behave yourself, Mother. This is home to a lot of nice people. It's home to me, too."

Her mother shook herself and pasted on a smile that could win an award. "Show me your castle, darling."

Tate grabbed only the essentials and followed them into the bakery. Ben was standing behind the counter.

"Katie, glad you made it back safely." He looked at her parents with a warm, genuine smile. "I'm Ben. Katie adopted me." He shook his head. "That's not quite the truth. Katie and Sage saved my life." He walked around the corner and hugged Sophia, who wasn't used to unexpected displays of affection. He then shook Katie's father's hand.

"Would you be a good man and fetch our bags from the trunk?" Tate palmed a hundred into Ben's hand.

"Dad, Ben is not your hired help."

Ben looked at the bill and handed it back. "I'd be happy to help with your bags, but I don't need your money." He pressed it back into Tate's hand. "I'm the richest man without it."

Katie felt a sense of pride toward Ben. He knew what had value—people. She wasn't responsible for his turn-around, but she was glad she got to see it. All she provided him was an opportunity.

That's exactly what Bea provided for her and Sage. What they did with her gift was up to them. Katie always hated when people accepted praise for the success of others. When her cousin Pat passed the bar exam, everyone told his parents they should be given praise for his accomplishment, but his parents didn't take the test. They didn't study for months on end. They didn't go to school to become a lawyer. Pat did, and he deserved the accolades. All his parents provided was an opportunity. Pat took that gift and turned it into something. It could have gone the other way.

"I'm going to leave you all for now. See you at the bar tonight?" Sage hugged Katie's mother and gave her father a nod.

"We'll be there." She guided her parents through the

bakery to the back staircase. She looked down at her mom's four-inch heels. "No elevator, sorry."

At the top of the stairs, she held her breath before she opened the door. "Before you go in, you need to know I love it here and there's nothing you can do or say to change my mind. I suggest you love it, too."

She swung open the door and walked into the tiny space. Being there with her parents made it even smaller. Her whole apartment would fit in their master bedroom at home.

Her mother's heels tapped across the floor. "It's ..." she turned to her husband, "charming. Right, Tate?"

He walked around the living room and stood at the window, looking out at Main Street. "Charming," he repeated.

Katie looked at her place through her mother's eyes. There were no hand-knotted rugs. No antiques—unless you counted the can opener on the kitchen counter. The furniture was blue. The walls were beige. The carpet was brown. The kitchen floor was fabricated plastic, not Italian tile. The counters came from a hardware store; they were not honed from stone carved from inside a mountain. Katie scanned her home. It wasn't much, but it was everything, and she loved it.

Ben pushed open the door with one of her parents' heavy bags. "Here you go. Where do you want them?" Ben had never been up here as far as Katie knew. He looked around the place like he was checking out a model home. "This place is amazing. No wonder you kids spend so much time up here."

Before her parents could question him, she said, "Ben is Bowie's father."

Both of her parents smiled. "Charming," they said in unison.

"First door on the left, Ben." Katie looked at her mother. "Did you bring anything less ... pretentious?"

"I have everyday clothes." As Ben came out of the hallway, her mother entered.

"See you later." Ben closed the door behind him.

Her father opened his arms like he was showing her something she hadn't seen. "This makes you happy?" He moved from the living room to the small galley kitchen.

"It's not the apartment. I like it, and it does make me happy, but it's the town and the people. They're real. When they smile, it comes from deep inside." Honesty was one of the most endearing qualities of the town. A pang of guilt rushed through her when she thought about how much she'd kept from the people of Aspen Cove.

"You bake?" Her father lifted the plastic wrap from a paper plate left on her counter. Inside were leftover poppy seed muffins.

"I do. I made those." She leaned against the counter and waited for his approval. It was funny because even though her mother was the tougher of her two parents when it came to acceptance, it was her father's blessing that meant more.

He took a bite and chewed. His eyes closed, like somehow that action helped him taste better. "I'll be damned. You can bake."

Pride filled her with warmth. "I make cookies, too. And mini cakes." She reached into the refrigerator and poured her father a glass of milk. "I haven't mastered big cakes yet. They always seem to fall on one side."

"Princess, I have no doubt those will be mastered soon. You may have a big heart, but you have a stubborn disposition. Your mother says you get it from me, but I'm not convinced."

"She gets what from you?" Sophia entered the kitchen wearing tailored slacks, a silk blouse, and patent leather pumps—her casual clothes.

"Her baking skills. Taste this." Tate handed his wife the second half of the muffin. "I'm going to change." He looked at Sophia, then at Katie. "Jeans okay?"

"Perfect, Daddy." She knew it was silly to use such a childish name for her father, but when she was with him, she always felt little.

Ten minutes later, her dad walked out looking like he belonged in Aspen Cove. Well ... almost, if it wasn't for the ten-thousand-dollar watch and two-hundred-dollar haircut.

Tate took a seat in the chair next to the couch. "When do we meet this boyfriend of yours? I thought he'd come with you to pick us up."

"He wanted to come, but I said no. I wanted you all to myself."

She knew it was a stupid answer because she'd brought Sage. Her parents didn't say anything to contradict her. By disappearing for months, she'd upset the balance in their totalitarian relationship. She was sure the minute she took charge of her life, her parents felt the repercussions of their total control parenting style.

"How are Isabella and Nick?" Both of her siblings were still in college. They were on the extended plan, and Katie hoped they'd found themselves in the time they'd spent away from home.

Her mom bubbled at the chance to talk about her kids. "Isabella is loving UCLA, and Nick is ready to come back to Dallas. They're both home for the summer but anxious to complete this journey in their lives."

Nick was attending NYU for a degree in business management. He'd take over the insurance business for her father when he was ready. Isabella, on the other hand, flitted between degrees. First, she tried art history, then ecology, now she was studying film. Like Katie, Isabella didn't have to work. Unlike Katie, Isabella didn't like to work.

Katie looked at the clock that sat on the end table. "Speaking of lives, do you want to come meet the people in mine?"

CHAPTER TWENTY-SIX

"Have a beer; it'll calm you down." Cannon pulled a lager into a frosty mug and set it in front of Bowie. "You look like a trapped animal."

He'd been walking the length of the bar for minutes. "I'm not used to being away from Katie this long." He cupped the frosted glass with his hands, but he didn't take a drink.

"If you're not drinking that beer, son, pass it down," Doc said. "And stop warming my beer with your hands."

Bowie slid the mug down the slick bar. When it landed in Doc's hand, the suds splashed over the side and onto the bar.

"Sage is back safe, so they're fine. She went home to check on Otis."

Bowie's phone buzzed in his pocket. He ripped it free and looked at Katie's message. "They're on their way." He'd never been so nervous about meeting anyone, but when Katie told him this morning her father was an insurance executive, he looked him up. Seems a donor heart wasn't the only information Katie had been withholding. Her father was one of the richest men in the United States.

"Give me a beer," he called to his brother.

"I just gave you one, asshole, and you gave it away." Cannon pulled another lager and set it in front of Bowie.

He lifted the mug. "Here's to everything."

"I'll drink to that," Doc said.

The door opened, and Bowie's heart stilled. Katie looked beautiful in her dress. The receding sun caught her blonde hair just right, making her look like she glowed. Dressed in his best jeans and a button-down shirt, Bowie rushed over to meet the parents.

He offered his hand to her mother first because he had manners and ladies always went first. "It's a pleasure to meet you, ma'am. I'm Bowie Bishop, your daughter's boyfriend." As he said the words, they sounded wrong because Katie was so much more than his girlfriend. She was his everything. He turned to her father, who'd been sizing him up since Bowie walked over to them. "Sir, it's also my pleasure to meet you. I've heard a lot about you."

That wasn't the truth exactly. He'd read a lot about the man—enough to make Bowie feel unworthy of Katie's love. He'd never be able to provide her with what she was used to, but he reminded himself all day that she was here because she found something she couldn't find anywhere else. He hoped it was him.

"Can I get you a drink?" Bowie led them to a table near the bar.

"I'll take whatever kind of whiskey you've got," Tate said.

"I'll take a glass of Duckhorn, please," Sophia replied.

When he gave her a confused look, Katie piped in, "She'll take the house cabernet."

When he walked to the bar, Cannon laughed. "You are so screwed," he whispered.

"Shut up, asshole, and get me the drinks," he whispered back. He knew his brother had heard the order. Outside of Doc, they were the only ones in the place.

Bowie returned with fizzy water for Katie, wine for her mother, and a glass of Jack for her father. He hated small talk, but he engaged in it anyway to break the ice.

"How was the flight?" He wanted to punch himself in the gut. He was sure the flight was great. How could it not be when it was a private jet?

"It was good. Do you know much about planes?"

Bowie sent up a silent *thank you* to the conversation gods. "I do. Planes have always fascinated me. I spent eight years jumping out of them."

"No kidding?"

"It's kind of a requirement to be a Ranger."

Tate looked at his daughter. "I didn't know he was a soldier, Katie."

She looked at her mom, who took a sip of the wine and made a face like she'd just eaten car wax. "I told Mama. I figured she'd pass that on."

Tate shook his head at his wife, then turned back to Bowie. "Seen any combat?"

The aches Bowie felt in his leg, his back, and his stomach were all reminders of how much combat he'd seen.

"More than I'd like to admit."

"He has a box of ribbons and medals." Katie threaded her fingers with his under the table. "He's a hero, Daddy."

"A hero?"

Bowie nudged Katie playfully with his shoulder. "She exaggerates."

"I do not. Seriously, he's got three of those Purple Heart ones."

Bowie was embarrassed because getting shot wasn't something he'd been proud of ever. Saving his people was where his sense of accomplishment rested.

Tate's hand slapped him on the back hard. "I'm so proud of you. I always wanted to serve, but my father had other plans for me."

"If you have a Purple Heart, then you've been injured." Sophia's voice held a drop of concern.

Bowie nodded his head. "Yes, ma'am. I've been shot and stabbed, but I made it back alive."

There was a moment of silence before Sophia spoke again. "This may seem insensitive, but it's my understanding that the heart in my daughter's chest once belonged to your fiancée."

Bowie had been expecting that. He was surprised it wasn't the first thing to come out of one of her parents' mouths.

"You're right. It was a shock, to say the least. Am I in love with your daughter's heart?" Bowie sat back and took a sip of beer. "I am, but not because it belonged to Brandy. I love your daughter because she has the biggest heart I know. It's *her* heart." He turned toward Doc. "This smart man I know asked me an important question, and I'll ask you the same. If your plane needed a new engine and your friend had one sitting unused in his garage and gave it to you, would it be his plane now, or still yours?"

Tate answered directly, "It's my plane."

Sophia nodded in agreement.

Bowie laid his hand over Katie's heart. "This is Katie's heart, and she owns mine, too."

They spent an hour at the bar, where they met most of

the town. No one comes to Aspen Cove unnoticed. While Katie's mother was on the less friendly side, her father quickly became a local.

Once they finished their drinks, they walked down the street to Maisey's Diner. Maisey had hired seasonal help. A woman named Meg took their order, but it was Dalton who delivered it. He always came out when his friends were around.

Katie rose to her feet and threw her arms around his neck once he dropped off the plates. "This is Dalton. He was my second friend in town."

If it were any other man, Bowie would have burned with jealousy, but he understood the relationship between the two of them was more like brother and sister.

He pulled up a chair while the group ate and talked about cooking and the town. It was funny to watch such a big man get excited about chicken-fried steak and Aspen Cove, but Dalton had had a tough childhood. If it weren't for Aspen Cove's mantra, "We take care of our own," Dalton and his mom wouldn't have made it. It was Doc who thought the diner would be a good idea. He and his wife financed the place until Maisey could pay off the note. Growing up, Dalton had always seemed more like a brother to Bowie, too. Hell, if his father moved forward with his feelings for Maisey, Dalton would be his stepbrother.

When a group of tourists walked in, Dalton said his goodbyes.

Tate gobbled up his plate of comfort food while Sophia picked at hers. "Do you eat here often?" she asked Katie.

"Often enough."

"That's probably why you've gained weight."

The back of Bowie's neck heated with irritation. Katie was perfect.

"I'm not overweight, Mama. Doc Parker checked me out a few weeks ago and said I was as healthy as a horse."

"You're trusting the word of a country doctor? You left the world's finest cardiologist to see a man who probably tends to people, pigs, and cows."

"And birds," Katie quipped.

Rumor had it, he mended a bird's wing at Sage's. The way they tell it, that was the start of their relationship. Bowie only wished he'd seen Sage with that bird nesting in her hair.

"Seriously," her mother said. "Staying here will be the death of you."

Tate laid his hand over his wife's. "Now, honey, you can see she's healthy and happy."

Katie took a minute, then addressed her mother. "Daddy can have the jet ready to leave in an hour if you don't stop. Aspen Cove isn't the death of me. It's the life of me."

When Tate pulled a large bill from his wallet to pay for dinner, Bowie stopped him.

"This is my treat, sir." He paid Meg and rose from the table. "I'll walk you and your parents across the street." It broke his heart to leave her alone with them. Her dad seemed fine, but her mother was something else.

Tate looked at his watch. "It's an hour later for us. Why don't you kids stay and enjoy each other?" He smiled at Katie. "I'll take your mother home and put her to bed. Maybe tomorrow she'll be rested and nicer."

Sophia gasped. "I'm nice. I'm just concerned about my daughter."

Tate laughed. "Look around you, Sophia. She can't get any safer here. Hell, her boyfriend is a damn Ranger. I think that earns him our trust." He helped his wife to her feet. "Is the door locked?"

Katie nodded but handed them her keys. "See you later, Daddy." She got up and kissed him on the cheek. "Thank you." She turned to her mother and did the same. "Love you, Mama."

As soon as they walked out the door, Katie pressed her face into his chest and breathed him in. "I'm so sorry. I told you she was impossible."

"Duchess, she's just being a mom." Bowie's mom had never been like that, but then again, he grew up in Aspen Cove.

They walked around town for the next hour until they got to an empty lot at the other end of Main Street.

"This used to be the park." He could still see the outline of where the baseball diamond had once been.

"What happened to it?"

He walked her to a grassy area and sat down, pulling her into his lap. His hands rested on her hips—his chin on her shoulder. He couldn't remember a time he'd felt more content. He would have loved to take her to his place and make love, but there was a little furry hellion waiting to make his debut at her birthday party tomorrow.

"When the paper mill went out of business, jobs dried up, and so did services. The town couldn't afford it all, so the Parks and Recreation Department folded." He'd been mostly grown by then, but he had fond memories of long days in this park.

She leaned against him and looked across the moonlit park. "What do the kids do now?"

"I imagine they stay inside and watch television or play video games."

"That's awful. They need a place to run and grow and play."

"I'd like to play." Bowie wrapped his arms around her middle and guided them both to the ground. "Maybe the kids make out in the tall grass like us."

He moved her to his side, so she faced him. She was so beautiful under the light of the moon. When he kissed her, she made that little moan that caused his blood to run like lava through his veins. No woman had ever made him so hot with a kiss.

CHAPTER TWENTY-SEVEN

"Happy birthday, sweetheart." Katie's father handed her a small white box.

Since Sage had taken her mom into the bed and breakfast for a tour, they had a minute to themselves. At the end of the dock of Bowie's childhood home, she opened her gift. On a bed of velvet sat a broken gold heart stitched together with the word "love."

"It's perfect."

She removed the necklace and turned around so her father could put it on her. It hung past the jagged scar that marred her chest—a scar she proudly wore now that she'd given her heart to Bowie.

"Where's the birthday girl?" Doc hollered from the end of the dock. He held a box in the air. "I brought gifts."

She looked at her dad.

"Go get your gift. It's your birthday." Katie raced to the end where Doc stood waiting.

"Don't open this in front of your father."

"Why?" She peeled back the corner and knew immediately. "Really, Doc? Condoms?"

"What do you get a girl who has everything?"

She threaded her arm through his and walked him to Sage's deck, where Cannon was barbecuing burgers and brats.

"Hey, birthday girl. Where's my brother?"

Katie looked around her. "He disappeared with your father a few minutes ago." She looked at the jumbo box of condoms. "Can you hide these for me?"

Cannon looked to where she had opened the end. "Ahhh. I'll put these away for later." He handed the barbecue tongs to Doc. "You're the new grill master."

Katie walked down the steps and looked at the water. Its surface rippled with the slight breeze. The aspens and pines shot up around the shore, enclosing the lake in a green hug. She'd been all over the world, but no place was as peaceful and homey as Aspen Cove.

"There you are." Bowie walked toward her with a gift in his hand. "You have to open this now. I'm not sure who's more excited, me or the gift."

She laughed because Bowie had once told her he wasn't good at riddles, and yet he managed to tell a few himself. Behind him walked Sage and Cannon, Ben, and her parents. Doc raised a beer and the tongs from his position on the deck. Maisey and Dalton pulled up the rear. In Dalton's hands was a cake on fire. It was amazing how much heat twenty-nine candles could create, but she felt it from a distance.

When the group came closer, they sang to her. She took a big breath and blew out the candles. It took her two tries, but she did it. Some would say she didn't earn her wish, but looking at the people surrounding her, she'd already been granted it.

"Who made the cake?" It was perfect. She knew there

wouldn't be an inch of frosting on one end to cover a mistake.

"Dalton made the cake," Bowie said. He stumbled sideways and almost dropped the box. "You need to open this now." The box bobbled in his hands again. "I'll hold it. You take off the lid slowly."

Katie gripped the lid. "Bowie Bishop, if something jumps out at me, you're in so much trouble."

"We'll see." He gave her a smile that could stop a weaker heart.

Afraid he was pranking her in some way, she leaned to the side before she pulled off the lid. "Oh my God." She lifted the brown bundle of wiggly fur into her arms. "You got me a puppy!"

Bowie threw the box to the ground and wrapped his arms around her and the puppy. "I gave you a child." He reached between them and lifted the dog tag that had "Bishop" etched into a metal bone.

"I love you." She tilted her chin up for a kiss.

Bowie met her in the middle and gave her a kiss she'd remember for a long time. She ignored the crowd around them and got lost in his love.

When Doc yelled, "The weiners are ready," everyone laughed.

A leash appeared from Bowie's back pocket, and he snapped it on Bishop's collar. "Dad's been teaching him to walk on the leash. He's a smart dog."

Katie smiled at him. "Of course he's smart. He's our son." She lowered Bishop to the ground and walked him to the deck where Sage had tables set up with salads and chips and buns. Everyone piled food onto their plates and claimed chairs.

Katie sat close to Bowie. Bishop lay at her feet. She was

giddy with happiness, but she was tired. All the excitement of the day had worn her out. She signaled to Sage, who walked right over.

"You need something, birthday girl?"

Katie felt the world tilt to the right. "I need to lie down for a minute. Can I use your room?" Sage had a full house this week due to the Fourth of July holiday.

A look of concern creased her brow. "Let's get you there."

Katie handed the leash to Bowie. "Can you take care of our child? I'm going to go inside for a few minutes."

"You okay?"

She nodded and pushed herself off the chair, but the world tilted again. "Bowie?" A flush covered her skin, and her knees buckled as she reached for him for stability.

In seconds, she was in his arms, and Sage was leading them into her and Cannon's bedroom. "I don't feel well."

Bowie put her on the bed and placed his hand on her forehead. He turned to Sage. "Get Doc, she's got a fever."

In seconds, the room was filled with people. It reminded Katie of the night before her surgery, when everyone came in to see her.

"Move away, everyone." Doc shuffled in and set his black bag on the nightstand.

"You do house calls?" Katie asked with a weak voice.

"Not if I can help it." He pulled the stethoscope from his bag. "You want an audience?"

Katie looked around the room. Her mother's hand covered her mouth. Her father seemed to hold Sophia up.

"I'm fine, just tired. Go enjoy the barbecue. I'll be out in a few minutes."

Katie's dad all but dragged his wife out of the room. The rest followed, except for Bowie.

"I'm staying." It was a statement of fact. He wrapped his big hand around her small hand and sat on the edge of the bed.

Doc lifted Katie's shirt and pressed the cold stethoscope to her chest. His head bobbed quickly while his eyes watched the second hand on his watch.

"Ticker is fine." He slung the instrument around his neck. "How have you been feeling?"

Katie scooted back and sat against the headboard—one similar to the one Cannon had made for Bowie and Brandy.

"I've been tired, but other than that, I've been great."

Bowie shook his head. "She threw up this morning."

Doc frowned. "Was it just this morning, or have you been sick before today?"

Bowie glared in her direction.

"I've been sick a few times."

"Mornings?"

"What? No?" She looked at Bowie, whose tawny skin turned ghostly white. "Seriously?"

Doc opened his bag and tossed the stethoscope inside. "Condoms have a failure rate of two to fifteen percent. Two if used properly."

Katie sat up. Her hands went to her stomach. Was it possible she was pregnant? "You think I'm pregnant?"

"Whoa, whoa," Bowie said. He rose from the bed and ran his hands through his hair. "She had her cycle."

"Normal?" Doc asked.

Katie shrugged. "I'm not sure what's normal. With my immunosuppressant drugs, nothing is ever normal."

"You're pregnant. I got you pregnant." The words were like a painful howl. "Shit. I've killed you."

"What? No, you did no such thing. You didn't have sex by yourself."

"Maybe he should have, and you wouldn't be in this predicament."

"Wait a minute," she yelled. "You don't know I'm pregnant."

The door opened wide, and Katie's mom stood there with a look of horror on her face. "What do you mean she's pregnant?" The last word came out in a cry.

"I'm not pregnant." Katie kicked her feet off the bed and tried to stand, but the change in position caused her to falter.

Bowie rushed to her side and scooped Katie into his arms. "She is pregnant. I know it."

"Only one way to find out." Doc closed his bag and walked to the door. "I'll meet you at the clinic."

When Doc disappeared down the hallway, Sophia surged toward Bowie. "If you really loved my daughter, you would have looked after her. Pregnancy is as good as a gun to her head."

Katie struggled from Bowie's arms and stood beside him. "Mother. I won't put up with you ruining everything for me. You need to leave now." Katie pointed a finger at the door.

"Me, ruin everything?" Sophia stood defiantly in front of Bowie. "He's ruining everything." Sophia pulled her hand back. When she swung it forward, she connected with Bowie's cheek with enough force to snap his head back. "If she's pregnant, I'll kill you myself."

"Sophia!" Tate stood in the doorway. "Come with me now."

Katie's mom walked toward her husband.

"Mama. You listen and listen well. I'd trade every minute of my life for one more with him."

The door closed behind them, and Bowie fell to his knees in front of Katie. "I'm so sorry."

Katie had only seen a man cry once. It was the day they wheeled her into the operating room. Her father had held her hand until the last minute. When she looked at him, his eyes couldn't hold the tears anymore. She looked down at Bowie, and his eyes looked the same.

"I can't live without you."

Katie dropped to her knees in front of him. "You don't have to live without me. Now go get our son and let's find out if you're going to be a daddy."

"Katie, you can't have this baby. Even you told me it wasn't recommended. It isn't safe. It isn't right."

"Bowie Bishop, have we done anything the right way?"

She leaned into his chest and breathed in his comforting scent. She'd never been so afraid, but it wasn't for her life she feared. It was for the life of the unborn child that might live in her womb.

CHAPTER TWENTY-EIGHT

Walking into Doc's was like walking in front of a firing squad. Bowie held Katie's hand in his. Although she was the picture of calm on the outside, the way her body shook gave her away.

"We'll take care of this so we can take care of you."

She shot him a look as deadly as an on-target bullet. "Haven't you learned anything?" She pulled her hand from his. "I can take care of myself."

She marched through the doorway that led to the examination room. He was hot on her heels, followed closely behind by Tate and Sophia. The latter had been tossing verbal grenades his way since she'd barged into Sage's room. No doubt Sophia had been standing there the whole time with an ear to the door.

"I know you can, but is it a bad thing that I want to care for you?"

"Care for me? No. Control me? Yes." She hopped onto the table. "If you want to help, tell Doc we're here."

Bowie nodded and walked out, but he heard Katie lay

into her mom. With Doc's shop empty, he didn't miss a word she said.

"You know why I left, Mama?"

"Yes. You wanted independence."

"That means making decisions for myself. If you want to be a part of my life, you need to step back and let me live it."

Their voices faded as Bowie ran upstairs to Doc's apartment. He had a setup similar to Katie's, although hers was by far nicer.

"You okay, son?"

Bowie plastered his body against the wall so Doc could slide past him in the narrow stairwell. "No, not really. I finally opened my heart and found love, and I've planted a death sentence inside her."

"Don't put the cart in front of the horse. Let's go see what's up. If she's pregnant, we'll concoct the best plan."

"She needs to get rid of that baby."

Doc expelled a heavy breath. "Have you learned nothing about women—that woman in particular? She doesn't want to be controlled; she wants to be supported. The decision is not yours. It's hers. If she's pregnant and wants to have that baby, she will. I've never met a more determined woman in my life. She rivals Phyllis for stubbornness." Doc sucked in a long breath and sighed out a loud exhale. "You love her?"

Bowie followed Doc down the stairs. "More than anything."

"Then you support her, no matter what."

Bowie swallowed the lump caught in his throat. "I will."

Doc swiped a few pregnancy tests from the shelf and walked into the room where Katie was still talking to her mom.

"You had your life, Mama. Let me have mine, no matter how long it is." She looked past her parents to Bowie. "I'm happy. I'm in love."

Bowie walked up to her and wrapped an arm around her shoulder. "You okay?"

A weak smile lifted the corners of her lips. "Yes, but can you help me clarify something?"

"Anything for you, Duchess."

She put her hand to her heart. "Was Brandy healthy?"

"Yes. She had no medical issues I knew about."

Katie reached her free hand to her mother's. "She was healthy, Mom. She woke up that day healthy and happy and in love."

Her eyes turned toward Bowie. He could see the love in her brilliant blue eyes, but he also saw sadness. He wasn't sure if it was because they were potentially facing a crisis or because she hated to bring up his wound. Knowing Katie, it was because she didn't want to hurt him.

"What's your point?" Sophia asked.

"My point is, no one is guaranteed anything. Brandy woke up to a normal day. She went about her business and climbed in a car to run an errand, and in the blink of an eye, her life was gone."

Bowie lifted his hand to the scar on his face. It was a visual reminder of how fast things could change.

"I have a donor heart. My life is risky, but no more at risk than any other life. So stop it." She looked around the room at her parents and him. "Shall I take this test and see where the next chapter leads?"

"I'm going to take blood and send it off to the lab, but let's see if we can't get a preliminary result with these." Doc handed her two different pregnancy tests and pointed to the bathroom.

Bowie dragged in several chairs from the hallway and lined them up against the wall for them to sit on. He took a seat and turned to Sophia.

"I really do love your daughter, and no matter what the outcome is, I will support her and take care of her."

Bowie could see the moment defeat and resignation claimed Katie's mom. Her features softened, and the visual daggers she'd been slicing through him dulled.

"I know you do. And she loves you. Not having a child of your own, you can't understand how I feel. I've spent twenty-nine years protecting her."

Tate cleared his throat. "Maybe it's time you spent the next phase of her life enjoying her. She's right, you know. Life isn't a guarantee. Live in the moment."

Katie emerged from the bathroom carrying two sticks. One in each hand. "What if we get mixed results?" She handed them to Doc, who set them on the counter and prepped to take her blood.

"I've got a third one out there we can use as a tiebreaker." He tied a rubber strap to her arm and had her hold on to a rubber ball. After a few taps at the crook, the needle went in the vial and filled up. Doc put on a Snoopy Band-Aid and popped a Life Saver into her mouth before she could say a word.

They waited. Katie and Bowie stared at the tests on the counter while Doc, Tate, and Sophia had their eyes on the clock. When the recommended time had passed, Doc read the results.

"It's unanimous." He raised the two tests, facing the group. One had two bright pink stripes, and the other clearly said pregnant 3+. "You can return your birthday gift for diapers since you won't be needing what I gave you for a while."

Bowie didn't know how to feel. A part of him wanted to crawl into a ball and die right there. Another part of him wanted to leap into the air with joy. His child was growing inside Katie, but could he risk ending one life in the hope of bringing another into the world? Then he remembered what she'd told them minutes before. Nothing in life was guaranteed.

"Oh my God ... I'm pregnant?" Gone was the weak smile, and in its place was the sun that burst forth from within her. "I never thought to put that on my bucket list." She reached for her bag and pulled out the journal where she recorded her dreams.

Bowie watched as she penned "have a baby" on a blank line.

Sophia stood and came over to her daughter. "Katie, are you—"

"Mama, I know what you're going to say. Don't."

Sophia gave her a grunt of frustration. "You're wrong. I was going to ask if you could clear a week next month so we can baby shop."

"Really?" Tears ran down Katie's cheeks.

"I'll send the jet," Tate said. He looked at Bowie. "Son, what are your intentions toward my daughter?"

"I intend to love her and care for her for the rest of my life."

"That sounds great, but will you marry her? We're old-fashioned that way."

"Daddy," Katie squeaked. "Bowie and I don't do anything the traditional way."

She was right. They'd kissed before they'd held hands. They'd slept together before they'd dated. They'd created a baby before they'd considered marriage. It was unconventional, but it worked for them.

"I'll marry her today if she'll have me."

"No way," Katie said with a hint of humor. Everyone looked at her in surprise. "If you think I'm going to make it easy on you by having my birthday and anniversary the same day, you're nuts. I'm not cheating myself out of an extra present or an extra day to celebrate."

Bowie cupped her face with his hands. "I love you. Every day is a day to celebrate, but I will marry you." He lowered one hand to her stomach. "I will be the best father and husband I can be."

Her father turned to Doc Parker. "What do I owe you, Doc?" Tate pulled out his wallet and tried to hand him a big bill.

Doc waved him away. "Nothing. Money isn't the most valuable currency here in Aspen Cove. We take care of our own."

"Surely, I can pay you somehow?"

Doc smiled. "Did I hear you have a jet?"

Tate laughed. "At your disposal."

KATIE'S PARENTS stayed long enough to visit her new cardiologist, Dr. Holland, in Copper Creek. After he gave her a full physical, he told everyone that although heart transplant recipients were at a high-risk for pregnancy, there was no reason to believe Katie wouldn't deliver a healthy child.

While he set up the ultrasound, he outlined the risks from infection to early delivery. He explained Katie's fever and the need to adjust her anti-rejection medications. When he gelled her stomach and placed the wand over her belly, the room fell silent except for the fast thumping beat that floated through the air.

All eyes went to the monitor where a clearly defined baby snuggled inside Katie's womb, its heartbeat a fast flicker on the screen.

"Your baby looks perfect," Doctor Holland said. "He or she is about eleven weeks along, weighs about an ounce, and is the length of your little finger."

Sophia burst into tears, followed by a laugh. "I told you you'd gained weight."

Everyone smiled at her joke.

"Can you tell what the sex is, Doctor Holland?" Tate asked.

"With this machine, it's too soon to say, but we should be able to see at your next appointment. That is, if you want to know."

Katie looked at Bowie. "You want to know?"

"Of course he wants to know," Sophia piped in. "It makes shopping easier."

"Let's decide then," Bowie said.

The doctor printed several copies of the baby photo and passed them out to everyone. Bowie folded his up and placed it in his wallet. Whereas he'd once kept a picture of Brandy to remember his past, this was a glimpse into his future.

"Let's go home," Katie said. "I miss our fur baby."

Turned out Otis was a fine father figure to Bishop. He'd taken to the puppy like they were raised together. Mike, on the other hand, wasn't a fan of the little furball, but that could be because Bishop was teething and decided Cannon's one-eyed cat was a good chew toy.

They dropped off Katie's parents at the airport, with a

promise to visit Dallas after the results of the next ultrasound.

On the way home, Bowie reached for Katie's hand. "This is all my fault."

"Are we back to that?"

Bowie thought back to his friend Trig's conversation about Sledge and his sand baby. "Yes, but not how you think. You got pregnant the first time I made love to you. I think I knew in my heart I loved you then, but I wasn't ready to admit."

"My heart has always loved you." There was a lot of truth to that statement. "What makes you think it happened on that night?"

"I used a condom that had been in my wallet for a year. It had been through the heat of the desert and a dozen sand-storms. When you warned me about heat breaking down latex, you were already pregnant."

She laid her hand over her belly. "A desert baby, huh?"

"Our desert baby," he replied.

CHAPTER TWENTY-NINE
TWENTY-SIX WEEKS LATER...

The frozen ground was unforgiving as the backhoe dug into the dirt.

"Are you sure this is the best time of year to be doing this?" Bowie asked as he wrapped his arms around her stomach. Katie felt the ripple of her child's swift kick move all the way to her back.

They stood with Bishop in the middle of the old park and watched the construction crew break ground. Katie wanted to pass her good fortune forward. Rather than use her trust fund to build a house or buy things she didn't need, she put a chunk of the money to community improvements like Hope Park.

She turned to her husband and looked into his eyes—eyes the color of a spring sky. "It has to be now. I want the children of Aspen Cove to have a place to play this summer." She walked to his right and pointed. "That's where the new baseball diamond is going." She turned and pointed behind them. "They're putting a jungle gym and swing sets over there." She pivoted to the left. "Right there will be a pavilion where the town can hold events like picnics or concerts."

"How much money is in this trust of yours?"

Because the money never mattered to her, she never brought it up until now. She had remembered the scripture recited at Bea's funeral that said something about money being used to do good. That people should give generously to those in need, always being ready to share what they have. Money in a trust didn't help anyone, but this park would.

"We're rich."

"How rich?" he asked her.

"We won't make the world's top ten, but we're okay."

"You want to spend your money on a park?"

She leaned in to him and breathed in his scent. "I want to invest in people. I want to pay the gifts given to me forward."

"You don't want a better house? A nicer car?" He looked to her wedding ring. "A bigger diamond?"

Though the diamond was small, the gesture was huge. She knew Bowie had spent every dime he had on this ring, and she'd wear it to her grave.

"I'm the richest woman in the world, and it has nothing to do with money."

She rubbed at the ache in her lower back. She was certain it was the cold January day that caused the persistent discomfort.

"Let's go home, and I'll make you your favorite tea."

"Home sounds good."

It was no longer the apartment above the bakery. Ben had taken that over and given them the lake house as a wedding gift. Most of Katie's favorite moments happened there. It was the place they created the new life inside her.

She had so many favorites with Bowie, but the day they stood on the end of the dock and said, "I do," topped her list. It was the same place where she threw an empty hook into the water and somehow caught the man of her dreams. Doc put on another hat that day and officiated over their vows.

Since then, she'd marked off hundreds of items from her bucket list, from roller skating to making love under the stars. In her twenty-ninth year, she'd lived a lifetime.

They walked together to the truck, and Bowie lifted her into the seat. Bishop curled up on the floorboard by her feet. He barely fit. The poor dog was convinced he was still a puppy.

When Bowie climbed in, he turned up the heat. "Let's get you defrosted." He leaned over to help with her seat belt and stopped. "Duchess?" His eyes went to the space between her legs. "You're melting."

Katie looked down just as a gush of warm water released. Bishop leaped from the floor onto the seat.

"Uh-oh."

Bowie grinned. "It's time."

Doctor Holland expected the baby to come around week thirty-seven, but they were turning the corner on week thirty-eight. All was right in the world except the incredible pain that gripped her middle.

Bowie immediately went into military mode. He was trained for high-stress situations, which was a good thing because Katie wasn't prepared at all. In that second, she felt completely unprepared to be a mother.

"Oh my God, what if I suck as a parent?"

She gripped the door handle and panted through the next contraction.

"You'll be an amazing mother. You already have the cookie-making down pat." Bowie dialed Sage and Cannon and told them to meet him outside for the handoff. Cannon would get Katie's suitcase, and Sage would take the dog.

Next he called Sophia and Tate and told them to get the jet ready. Their grandchild was coming. Much to Sophia's disappointment, they didn't know the sex. The baby was a gift, and it didn't matter if it was a boy or a girl. It's not like they could send it back.

The final call, which should have been the first call, was to Dr. Holland, who promised everything would be ready when they arrived.

When they got to Copper Creek General Hospital, Dr. Holland was waiting with a wheelchair.

"How are you doing there, Mom?" he asked Katie. Then he turned to Bowie. "What about you, Dad? Ready to meet your baby?"

Bowie relayed pertinent information while Katie puffed through another contraction. Four hours that seemed like a lifetime later, her parents rushed into the delivery room. They stood by her head while Bowie coached her through the last phases of labor. Because she was a high-risk pregnancy, at least a half dozen specialists were standing nearby. Katie was grateful for their presence but confident she wouldn't need them. She had Bowie, she had her parents, and she had the strongest, most loving heart in the world.

When Dr. Holland told her to push, she felt an extra surge of strength. Ten minutes later, Sahara Brandelyn Bishop was born. When she grew old enough to understand, Bowie and Katie would tell her about all the people who made it possible for her to exist. How dreams can come true and how the only currency worth collecting is love.

She looked down at her daughter, who had eyes like her father and a scream loud enough to wake the dead, and she smiled. In her mind, she checked off another item from her bucket list.

As she took a deep breath, she felt warmth flood her chest. Call her crazy, but she knew Brandy was with them. Looking down on them with love. She was certain her gift would beat for years to come.

Katie reflected on the last few months. She was certain of so many things when she arrived in Aspen Cove, but she'd been taught many lessons along her journey.

Hope didn't come in a pink envelope. It was visible in the eyes of the man who loved her and in the heartbeat of the child in her arms.

Prince Charming may ride a Harley, but he also drove a truck and drove her crazy.

Secrets were never best left unspoken. The truth set her free.

There was a final thing she'd learned, maybe the most important since her arrival. Being independent didn't mean being alone. It meant surrounding herself with people who cared, people who valued her opinion, and who celebrated her successes along with her failures.

Bowie looked down at his wife and child. She saw the tears in his eyes—tears of joy.

"Your bucket list is empty," he said. "What's next?"

While Tate and Sophia counted Sahara's fingers and toes, Katie giggled. "How about a boy?"

ALSO BY KELLY COLLINS

An Aspen Cove Romance Series

One Hundred Reasons

One Hundred Heartbeats

One Hundred Wishes

One Hundred Promises

One Hundred Excuses

One Hundred Christmas Kisses

One Hundred Lifetimes

One Hundred Ways

One Hundred Goodbyes

One Hundred Secrets

One Hundred Regrets

One Hundred Choices

One Hundred Decisions

One Hundred Glances

One Hundred Lessons

One Hundred Mistakes

One Hundred Nights

One Hundred Whispers

One Hundred Reflections

One Hundred Intentions

One Hundred Chances

One Hundred Dreams

GET A FREE BOOK.

Go to www.authorkellycollins.com

ABOUT THE AUTHOR

International bestselling author of more than thirty novels, Kelly Collins writes with the intention of keeping love alive. Always a romantic, she blends real-life events with her vivid imagination to create characters and stories that lovers of contemporary romance, new adult, and romantic suspense will return to again and again.

For More Information
www.authorkellycollins.com
kelly@authorkellycollins.com

ACKNOWLEDGMENTS

Where do I start? There are so many people that must be recognized. I always say it starts with an idea but that's not actually true. It starts with the love and support of a village. Family and friends and fans are what fuel the words. Without them it's like owning a car and having no gas.

Special thanks to my writing bestie Mel, who never fails to be a cheerleader no matter what.

Hugs and that mushy stuff to everyone in Kelly Collins' Book Nook and Kel's Belles. They all play well in the sandbox and help me make the tough choices like what couple to put on the cover.

Speaking of covers. These covers were not what I envisioned when I wrote the books. When *One Hundred Reasons* won in Kindle Scout, it was suggested strongly that I put a couple in scene in Aspen Cove and so a new vision had to be created in record time. Thank you Victoria Cooper Art for coming to my rescue.

Thanks to the ladies who proofread this book. Judy and Sabrina, I'm grateful for the hours you devote to making sure my work is the best it can be.

Last but never least, I thank you the reader for being loyal fans. Because you continue to ask for more, I continue to write. I hope you enjoy your time in Aspen Cove. There's so much more to come.